If Pigs Could Fly

IF PIGS COULD FLY

Stories by
DAVID ARNASON

TURNSTONE PRESS

Turnstone Press gratefully acknowledges the assistance of the Canada Council and the Manitoba Arts Council.

The following stories, or versions of them, have been broadcast on CBC Radio, either regionally or nationally: "Badger and Fox," "Goldilocks and the Health Care System," "The Pirates," "Golden Boys," "The Man Who Stole Recess," "The Silver Lining," "The Land of Plenty," "The Birthday Party," "If Pigs Could Fly," "Puddle and Pond" and "The Peaceable Kingdom."

"At Babi Yar" and "Once in a Small Bar in Odessa" have previously appeared in *Border Crossings* magazine. "At the Grave of Taras Shevchenko" previously appeared in *Prairie Fire* magazine. "Me and Alec Went Fishing with Rimbaud" and "Torch Song" are from *Beyond Borders* (Turnstone Press and New Rivers Press, 1992).

Design: Manuela Dias

This book was printed and bound in Canada by Kromar Printing Ltd. for Turnstone Press.

Canadian Cataloguing in Publication Data

Arnason, David, 1940–

If pigs could fly

ISBN 0-88801-202-0

I. Title.

PS8551.R765I4 1995   C813'.54   C95-920221-8
PR9199.3.A75I4 1995

for Wayne Tefs

CONTENTS

Political Fables

Badger and Fox

 ell," said Fox. "I have done it at last. I have balanced my budget. Everything on the right side of the ledger is the same as everything on the left side of the ledger, and there is an equal amount of red ink and black ink."

"That is very fine," said Badger. "If you're through, perhaps we could go down to Farmer Gary's meadow and eat a couple of mice. Or perhaps we could find a splendid fat gopher. Or a mole. I saw some very nice moles there just the other day."

"Would you please stop thinking of your stomach," said Fox. "You have far more stomach than is good for you. I believe you could do with some restraint. Perhaps you could reduce your intake of squirrels, gophers, birds, and other small animals in the interest of the meadow as a whole."

"Now there's where you're wrong," Badger said. "To be a badger is to be an eater of small animals. I understand that might be seen as deplorable from the point of view of a small animal, but look at it this way. The small animals may eat as many badgers as they like. That they do not eat badgers is simply a lack of initiative on their parts and not my fault. What seems like a lack of balance, is in fact Nature's Way."

"A solid argument," replied Fox, who liked a juicy gopher or a tender mouse as much as anybody. "Nevertheless, I think a balanced budget is a very beautiful thing, and I also think everyone should be required to have one."

"Taking into account the fact that some of us are hard-working badgers and some of us are merely lazy and un-employed mice without initiative."

"Yes," said Fox. "Taking that into account. I propose there-fore that we legislate that all the creatures of the meadow must from now on balance their budgets."

"Can we do that?" asked Badger.

"Why not?" Fox replied. "You are a badger and I am a fox. The wolves in some of the meadows to the south of us have done just that, and it has done wonders for the deer population. We could offer just the same advantages to our own mice and gophers."

So Fox proposed the motion and Badger seconded it and they both voted in favour and went out to inform the other denizens of the meadow.

The first person they met was Old Mother Hubbard with a basket of goodies and her dog. Mother Hubbard was fat and good-natured, and she invited them in for lunch, but her dog was thin and bad-tempered. It growled at Fox and Badger. Mother Hubbard ordered him to be quiet, and he was.

Then Old Mother Hubbard opened her basket and set the table with a wonderful spread of pâtés and baguettes and Black Forest ham and ice cream and cake. As they feasted, Fox explained his plan for a balanced budget. Mother Hubbard was delighted.

"It is just the way I operate, myself," she exclaimed. "You see this fine dog I own. At one time I didn't believe I could afford a dog, but since I have balanced my budget I have no difficulty at all." She went to the cupboard.

"I'll just give him a bone," she said, but when she got there, the cupboard was bare, and so she took him out and tied him to a tree instead, where he howled dismally.

"You see," she said, "when there is a bone in the cupboard, I give it to him, and when there is none, I do not."

"Has there ever been a bone there?" Badger asked. The dog was clearly hungry and had begun to look a little mutinous.

"Not so far," said Mother Hubbard. "But that is not to say there will never be a bone there. In the meanwhile, sacrifices must be made, and I am prepared to make them." She finished off a drumstick and threw the bone into the garbage.

"A very fine woman," Badger said as they walked on a little later. "Is that the way you balance your budget, Fox?"

"Not exactly," Fox replied. "It is easy to balance your budget when nothing comes in and nothing goes out. It is a bit harder when a great deal goes out and very little comes in, as is the situation in my case."

"You are a gentleman," Badger said. "A man of property. A man of ease. But how did you accomplish a balanced budget? I think none of us expected it from you. If I remember, you had a small inheritance that disappeared rather quickly."

"Yes, yes, let's not bother about that," Fox said. "It is simply a matter of proper accounting. First, you will remember that I ran a substantial deficit last year."

"Yes, indeed," Badger replied. "It was in all the papers."

"Well, I simply took half of this year's deficit and assigned it to last year. Last year's deficit is now much larger than it was, but since last year has passed, it causes no problem to anyone."

"Brilliant!" said Badger.

"And you remember my brother the gambler? Well, he contributed the rest of the money needed to entirely wipe out the deficit. And so my budget is balanced."

"As I remember," Badger said, "your gambling brother had no money."

"You are right," said Fox. "He had to borrow it. But now it is he that has the deficit and not me."

"I see," said Badger, though the finances had become a little more complicated than he liked. And anyway, they had reached the big oak tree that stands by the pond in Farmer Gary's meadow.

Fox rang the bell that hung from the tree and that was used to call all the creatures of the meadow together. In no time they were there, frogs and muskrats and rabbits and birds and squirrels and mice and a couple of particularly plump and juicy gophers.

"My fellow denizens of Farmer Gary's meadow," Fox began, "I am here to inform you of my wonderful new plan for a balanced budget. From now on, every one of you will be required to balance his budget, and if you fail to do so, your salary will be cut by forty per cent. This of course will also apply to me."

At first, many of the animals applauded the plan. They had worked hard gathering seeds for the winter, and they didn't like the idea that other animals were freeloading on their work.

But Fox went on. "Farmer Gary's meadow is a great place for the growing of seeds. It has justly been called the bread-basket of the entire farm. Now, since we have so many seeds, we will take half of your seeds so that we may exchange them with the wolves to the south of us for more meat."

A number of the animals grumbled at that, since they themselves did not eat meat, but Badger showed them a study he had written that showed that meat eaters were responsible for all the wealth in the meadow. It was their selfless avoidance of seeds that permitted the others to thrive.

"And beyond this," Fox went on, "out of the goodness of our hearts, we are going to allow each of you to have ten days off without pay. Nobody will be required to work during those days."

Then a small mouse who didn't understand the intricacies of economics said, "But if we don't work, we will starve even if the budget is balanced."

It was the last straw. Fox looked at Badger, and Badger looked at Fox. They pounced at the same moment, and each caught a plump gopher, a sleek young mouse and a delicious tiny bird.

As they walked back home, Badger told Fox, "You are certainly right about trying to strike a balanced budget. The seed eaters so outnumber the meat eaters that we have hardly even begun to redress the balance."

They licked their lips and agreed that they would come back the very next day and carry on with their good work.

GOLDILOCKS AND THE
HEALTH CARE SYSTEM

 'm sorry," the doctor told Goldilocks. "I'm afraid I'm going to have to operate. Please check into the Health Sciences Centre on the fourteenth."

Goldilocks was new to Manitoba. She'd just arrived from someplace else a week ago, and had gone to the doctor for the medical she needed for her new job.

"I wonder," said Goldilocks, "whether you might possibly have time to explain what's wrong with me, Doctor Filmon, and just what sort of operation I will have."

"I'm sorry," the doctor said. "I'm a very busy man. Already I am an hour behind and the waiting room is filled with people. Perhaps if you were a man I could explain it all to you, but under the circumstances, you will simply have to wait until the operation."

Goldilocks had always thought of herself as a good little girl, and so she said nothing, but went home and presented herself at the Health Sciences Centre on the fourteenth. She went to the desk marked Receptionist, but there was no one there. A computer flickered green and red lights.

"How can I help you?" the computer asked in a slow tinny voice.

"I've come for an operation," Goldilocks said.

"Have you had this operation before?" the computer asked.

"I don't believe so," Goldilocks answered. "I've never had an operation before."

"Put your medical card in the slot," the computer told her, and it flashed its light in a way that Goldilocks thought was hostile. "And kindly deposit the user's fee in the receptacle."

The only receptacle Goldilocks could see was what appeared to be an old cookie jar. She deposited twenty dollars.

"Kindly deposit the user's fee," the computer told her again. She gave it another twenty, but it was still not satisfied. At seventy-five dollars, it started to hum, and it spat out a record of every visit she had ever made to a doctor since the day of her birth. The bill was for thirty-seven thousand dollars. The computer instructed her that arrangements could be made for an easy time-payment plan.

"But what do I do now?" Goldilocks asked.

"725-364," the machine told her, but no matter what else she asked it, it refused to speak.

"I will find a human to speak to," Goldilocks told herself, "and then it will be all right. I must be able to find a friendly nurse."

And she set off down one of the corridors.

"This is a long and dark hallway," she thought, "but I can make out footprints painted on the floor." She followed them to an elevator, and on an impulse, she went up to the seventh floor.

The hallways on the seventh floor were as dark and empty as those on the ground floor.

"If I am to have an operation," Goldilocks thought, "then I had better find myself a bed." There were rooms on both sides of the hallway, but not one had a bed in it. Finally she came to an area with a sign that said Nursing Station. On the desk were three bowls of thin porridge.

"I am so hungry," she said to no one in particular, "that I

had better eat something." And she tried the one that said Poppa Bear on the bowl. The gruel was thin and vile tasting, and much too cold, and she spat it out. Then she tried the bowl that said Mamma Bear, but it was equally thin and vile and cold, and she spat that out too. The third bowl said Baby Bear, and though the gruel in that bowl was as thin and as vile as the gruel in the other bowls, she ate it all up.

Goldilocks was beginning to feel tired.

"Fortunately," she told herself, "there are three chairs right over here, and there's writing on them. Mamma Bear, Poppa Bear and Baby Bear. I wonder if I'm in the right place. This appears to be a veterinary hospital, and that would account for the absence of beds." She tried all three chairs, but they were all so rickety that she decided to sit on the floor instead.

A moment later a woman in a white dress with white shoes came in and sat down on the floor right next to her.

"Excuse me," Goldilocks asked. "Is this a veterinary hospital?"

"Veterinary hospital indeed," the woman in white said indignantly. "This is the Health Sciences Centre, the most important and finest hospital in all of Manitoba."

"Where are the beds?" Goldilocks asked.

"Beds indeed," the woman replied. "Do you think in a place as busy as this there is any time to lie about in beds?"

The woman seemed to take offence very easily, so Goldilocks said gently, "I'm here for an operation. With Doctor Filmon."

"What are they taking out of you?" the woman asked.

"I don't know," Goldilocks replied.

"I don't suppose it matters," the woman went on. "There are plenty of things inside a woman that can be removed. Far more than necessary. Did you say Doctor Filmon?"

"Yes."

"He's gone to Tennessee. Or Texas. Someplace where they need doctors."

"But who will do my operation?"

"Somebody. Just stay here lying on the floor and somebody will come by and remove something."

9

Goldilocks didn't much like the thought of some stranger operating on her, though when she reflected, she actually didn't know Doctor Filmon very well either.

"Are you a nurse?" she asked the woman in white.

"Well, as to that," the woman replied, "the question is not that easy. I was a nurse. A licenced practical nurse. But I've been legislated out of existence." And she began to weep softly.

"There, there," Goldilocks said. "You can't have been legislated out of existence. The government would never do a thing like that. Besides, look at yourself. You're as solid as me."

The nurse began to weep more loudly, and Goldilocks noticed that she was beginning to disappear. First her legs went. Then her arms. Finally only her head was left, floating about two feet above the floor.

"Please don't go," Goldilocks said. "I didn't mean to offend you. Or if you must go, tell me where I can find my hospital bed."

All that was left of the nurse was one eye and her mouth. The eye winked a horrible wink and the mouth said, "Try the orchard," and then they both disappeared. Goldilocks was left alone, but she noticed a small doorway that she hadn't seen before.

She went through the door and found herself in an orchard. There were peach trees and pear trees and orange trees and grapefruit trees, but none of them had any leaves or any fruit. One withered tree in the corner had a crabapple on it. Three bears were sitting near it in front of a small fire.

"Excuse me," Goldilocks said. "Is this the orchard?"

"Yes," said Poppa Bear. "I suppose you're right. It appears to be an orchard."

"But there is no fruit," Goldilocks said. "Orchards are supposed to be rich, lush places, but here there is only one sickly crabapple."

"Why, you're right," Mamma Bear said. "This is a very poor place indeed."

"That's because this is Manitoba," Baby Bear piped up. "We can't afford rich things. We must exercise restraint."

"Do you live here?" Goldilocks asked. "I mean permanently?"

"Oh, no," Poppa Bear said. "We live wherever it is best for bears to live. And just now we are finishing off a small picnic, and as soon as we put the fire out, we'll be moving on."

"I don't suppose you'd have room for me?" Goldilocks asked.

"Why certainly," cried Mamma Bear. "We can all live happily ever after as soon as we find the place where all the doctors and nurses have gone."

And that's what happened.

THE PIRATES

t was a hard squall, a real nor'easter," Captain Toban told the twelve people gathered around the table in the small room in Ottawa. "We wuz sailin' on a broad reach round the cape just on the northwest corner of Newfoundland when she struck. 'T'was about seven o'clock in the evening and we'd just handed the boyos their evening ration of rum when the wind shifted and the sky went black. Then the rain came in sheets and the wind howled, and the waves were twenty feet high. 'Get below,' I shouted to the men, and I strapped Lloyd to the mizzenmast, and I strapped meself to the wheel and we rode her out."

"Why Lloyd?" Paul asked. "Why did you strap Lloyd to the mizzenmast?"

"He was in the way," the Captain answered. "He's always in the way with his soft landlubber's ways."

"I think I know what you mean," Paul said. "Go on with the story."

"Well, anyway," the Captain went on, "we took all the fury the sea could offer, and ye know, boys, there's no fiercer sea than off the coast of Newfoundland. Finally, she blew herself out and the sky lightened, though there was a terrible fog that morning."

"I was in a fog once," David Dingbat said. "I was walking down Yonge Street, when this terrible fog . . ."

"You're still in a fog," Jean told him. "Stop interrupting and let the Captain tell his story."

"Well, like I said, I was just about to unbatten the hatches and let the men out when I heard this strange hissing noise. At first I didn't know what it was. I thought perhaps one of the compressors was leaking, but finally I figured it out. Spanish."

"No," one of the ministers gasped. "Not in Canadian waters."

"Not exactly," the Captain admitted. "But nearly. A mere four hundred miles away."

"But why were they there?" Paul asked. "What did they want?"

"The very question I asked myself. I listened carefully. As we inched toward them, I could hear them singing *Malaguena*, and only moments later came the sounds of castanets and guitars. I could hear laughter and dancing."

"Surely not laughter and dancing so close to the Canadian coast?" Paul said. "Damn it, there are international treaties about that sort of thing."

"Laughter and dancing it was," the Captain said. "It made no sense at all until we got a little closer and I could see the crew. They all held small white fishes in their hands, and were eating them as they danced."

"Not . . . ?" the others gasped.

"Yes," the Captain said. "Turbot. They were crazed on turbot. It's a well-known fact that Spaniards cannot handle turbot. A single bite and they're dancing and singing and playing guitars as if there were no tomorrow."

"What did you do?" Jean asked.

"There was only one thing I could do. I had to save them. First, we moved in on them quickly before they knew we were there, and we cut their nets so that they couldn't catch any more turbot, and the source of their mania was gone. Then we fired a shot across their bow and we forced them into the harbour at St. John's. I'm proud to say that by the time we reached shore, not a single one of them was singing or dancing or laughing. They could have walked down any street in Canada and passed as Canadians."

"You did well," Jean said. "You're a true Canadian. After what you've done, the Canadian tourist will be welcomed in Madrid."

"Aye, Jeanie Me Bucko, and that minds me of another tale," Captain Toban went on. "It was off the Alaska Panhandle. We'd been sailing on a broad reach when the squall struck, a real sou'wester. 'T'was about seven o'clock in the morning and we'd just handed the boyos their morning ration of rum when the wind shifted and the sky went black. Then the rain came in sheets and the wind howled, and the waves were twenty feet high. 'Get below,' I shouted to the men, and I strapped Lloyd to the mizzenmast, and I strapped meself to the wheel and we rode her out."

"And you had Lloyd again, did you?" asked Paul.

"Well, he's a hard man to get rid of," the Captain said.

"And don't I know it," Paul answered. "Why, I remember like it was yesterday. I was working in my office, dismantling the social security system when Lloyd up and . . ."

"And the wind she blowed and blowed and the waves were thirty feet high. And I said to myself, 'Captain,' I said,' if you pull through this one, you got to devote the rest of your life to human betterment.' Well no sooner did I say that than the wind slowed and the waves eased, and what should we see right before us but a boatload of Alaskan fishermen. I invited them aboard to parley about fishing in international waters when what do you think I saw?"

"What?" Jean asked.

"Diseased. Every man and boy of them come down with the salmon disease. Their captain was already going green around the gills, and every single member of the crew was sockeyed."

"Excuse me," Paul said. "What was that disease?"

14

"Salmonella," the Captain said. "You get it from eating too much salmon. It's not a pretty sight. The worst is that it's addictive, like a powerful drug. Once you get to eating salmon, you can't stop. You want more and more. You become insatiable. You can't help yourself."

"I thought salmonella was caused by uncooked hamburgers and chickens and things," Paul said.

"That's what they tell you in Ottawa," the Captain said. "But let me warn you. Never eat salmon if it's gone pink in the can. Whamo. Salmonella."

"So what did you do?" Jean asked.

"What could I do?" the Captain answered. "I couldn't let the entire state of Alaska come down with salmonella, could I? I told them they'd have to stop fishing."

"And did they?" Jean asked.

"Well, not right away. Once you're hooked on salmon it's a hard habit to kick, and they've been pretty resistant."

"So what did you do?" Paul asked.

"Well, so far, we captured one ferry and held it until everybody aboard had passed the salmon through their systems, and then when we thought it was safe, we sent it on to the States."

"I expect they're grateful for that," Jean said.

"Well, not so far," the Captain replied. "But then the Americans are not a particularly grateful bunch. I expect they'll come around once they realize we're only stopping them from fishing for their own good. And speaking of ingratitude, that reminds me of another tale."

"Talking about ingratitude," Jean said, "have I told you about Sheila Copps and the . . . ?"

"It was on Lake Winnipeg," the Captain said. "We'd been sailing on a broad reach when the squall struck, a real nor'wester. 'Twas about twelve o'clock noon and we'd just handed the boyos their afternoon ration of rum when the wind shifted and the sky went black. Then the rain came in sheets and the wind howled, and the waves were twenty feet high. 'Get below,' I shouted to the men, and I strapped Lloyd to the

15

mizzenmast, and I strapped meself to the wheel and we rode her out."

"Lloyd?" Paul asked.

"Like always. He'd figured out a way to wean the fishermen off unemployment insurance and they were in a pretty foul mood. This time I left him strapped to the mizzenmast."

"Good idea. Jean, can we get a mizzenmast erected in the House?"

"I tink so."

"Good."

"Anyway, we were there to investigate the tullibee problems. As you probably know, the tullibee stocks are in dire danger. As Minister of Fisheries and Captain of the SS *Canada,* I saw my duty and I saw it clear. We've always claimed Lake Winnipeg as Canadian waters."

"Now do we, Captain?" Jean said. "That's very interesting."

"It's Lloyd's idea," Paul told them. "Frankly, I think it's a mistake."

"At any rate," the Captain went on, "the storm broke and the waters grew calm. We were lying to the east of George's Island, and I scoured the horizon with me telescope. Illegal tullibee fishermen. I could see that in a moment. Over on George's Island I could see a whiff of smoke where they were smoking their ill-gotten gains. Me heart fairly thumped with rage."

"And what did you do?" Paul asked.

"I sailed right over to the ship, the MS *Filmon,* and shouted, 'Avast ye lubbers. By what right do you fish illegally for tullibee in these waters?' Well, their captain was as bold as brass.

" 'Look,' he said, and showed me a fishing licence from the Manitoba Government, and he went on fishing.

" 'These here are Canadian waters,' I told him.

" 'I know,' he shouted back, but he went on fishing.

"Finally, I could stand it no more. I readied the big guns, and I blasted him out of the waters. Then there were more ships, the MS *Stefanson,* the MS *Gilleshammer,* the MS *McCrae.*

All busy depleting the Canadian tullibee stocks. I blasted them all out of the water, I'm proud to say."

"Uh, Captain," Paul interjected. "I hope you won't take offence, but I believe that Manitoba is a part of Canada."

"What?"

"That's what Lloyd says."

"Nonsense."

"Isn't that true, Jean?"

"I don't know. I tink I heard something about that one time."

Somebody handed the Captain a map, and he studied it intently.

"Look, here, it's the one in the middle, the funny-looking one," Paul said, and he tried to point out Manitoba on the map, but it was too late. The Captain's eyes had begun to glaze over.

"Did I ever tell you about that time on Lake Ontario when I sunk the German U-boat? We were sailing on a broad reach . . ."

Golden Boys

nce upon a summer's night in the city of Winnipeg, a starship of the XN class of the Jovian starfleet hovered over the Manitoba legislature. The captain, a Jovian from the planet PR36, opened the bay doors, lowered the transform receiver and pressed the lift button on his console. A moment later the Golden Boy had disappeared from the dome of the legislature and reappeared in the bay of the starship.

Harvey was sitting on the grounds of the legislature, just finishing a bottle of Calona Royal Red wine, which he had hidden inside a brown paper bag.

"Holy cow," he said. "Did you see that?"

There was no answer, because there was no one else there. Harvey picked up his bottle of wine and examined it.

"You're not doing me any good," he told the bottle. "No good at all." And he dropped his bottle and staggered down to Broadway Avenue.

Before Harvey had even reached Broadway, the Jovian starship had slipped into warp mode and was entering the Omega galaxy, a hundred million light-years away. The captain had just brought out a bottle of starbeet champagne, the drink of choice on planet PR36, when his radio crackled.

"Starship B12, please report," a sharp voice commanded.

"Mission successful," the captain said. "We have the Golden Boy from the planet Earth."

"What?" the voice on the other end shrieked. "What did you say?"

"I said, we have the Golden Boy from the planet Earth."

"You fools," the voice shouted. "You were supposed to get the Golden Toy from the planet Perth. You've done it all wrong."

"What shall we do?"

"Return it, you fools. Then go get the Golden Toy from the planet Perth. You aren't even in the right galaxy."

"Sorry," the captain said. He slipped back into warp mode and seconds later he was orbiting Earth.

"Where did we get this?" he asked the onboard computer. Unfortunately they had passed through a region of no depth on their return in warp mode, and, of course, the computer was now off by two and a half degrees.

"Node 2100, axis 42B," the computer said. The captain opened the bay doors, lowered the transform sender and pushed the button on the console marked Replace. The Golden Boy disappeared from the bay of the starship and reappeared on top of a trapper's cabin two hundred miles northwest of Gillam, Manitoba. Then the captain consulted the computer once more, put his starship into warp drive and disappeared from the universe.

Near Gillam, a young boy named Paul just happened to be celebrating his thirteenth birthday. The elders of his tribe had sent him out on his own into the forest to fast, and he was just approaching the cabin. The last thing his father had told him was that young men entering manhood often had visions, and these visions were important. You could learn about your future if you handled them properly.

"That's interesting," Paul said to himself as the Golden Boy appeared on the roof of the cabin. "This must be my vision. I'll get a good night's sleep and talk to it in the morning."

The first person to notice the next morning that the Golden Boy was gone was the Premier.

"They have probably taken it away to clean and polish it," he thought. "Nobody ever tells me anything around here anymore. Perhaps I've been Premier too long."

"Where is the Golden Boy?" his secretary asked as the Premier walked into his office.

"I expect they've taken it out for cleaning," he told her. "I'll have to ask the Minister for Statues and Objects of Art."

"There's a man named Harvey out in the hallway. He says it was stolen by aliens."

"Tell him it's out for cleaning," the Premier said, and he sat down to read some very dull papers about the single tax.

All day people phoned to ask about the Golden Boy. The Premier's secretary told them all that it was out for cleaning, and they all seemed satisfied with that explanation, except Harvey.

"There are aliens out there stealing statues," he told his travel agent. "Lord knows what they'll be doing next. I want to go to the loneliest place on earth."

The travel agent looked it up in his book, and gave Harvey a one-way ticket with Northern Bush Plane Services. He would be taken to a trapper's cabin two hundred miles northwest of Gillam.

In the meantime, Paul was having trouble with his vision. The vision wouldn't speak to him. He had made it a list of questions.

"What does the future hold for me?

"Why is the sky blue?

"Will I be able to go to law school and help my people?

"Who will win the Stanley Cup?"

No matter what he asked the vision, it did not reply.

"This is no good," Paul said to himself. "If this vision doesn't give me some answers I'll starve to death before my fast is over."

The next day it was the same. He asked the Golden Boy a series of questions, but the Golden Boy would not respond.

By the third day, Paul was really hungry. The Golden Boy would not even tell him the time. Paul was about to move on and try to find a better vision when he looked up into the sky and saw a man dangling from a parachute.

"Good," he thought. "Perhaps this new vision will have a few answers."

Back in Winnipeg, the Premier bumped into the Minister for Statues and Objects of Art.

"Where's the Golden Boy?" he asked.

"I heard you'd sent him out to be cleaned," the Minister replied.

"I thought you'd sent him out," the Premier answered.

"Not me. But whoever did had better get him back. It's only a couple of days until Manitoba's one hundred and twenty-fifth birthday party, and we can't celebrate it without the Golden Boy."

"We could advertise on television and in the newspapers," the Premier said. "Somebody must know where he is."

"If we advertise, then the media will blame us," said the Minister. "How are people going to trust the government if we lose the Golden Boy right off the top of the legislature?"

"You're right," said the Premier. "We'll have to ask my secretary. She's the only one who knows what's going on around here."

So they asked the secretary, and she said, "Get the RCMP to find Harvey. He knows what has happened."

When the RCMP couldn't find Harvey on his usual bench in front of the legislature, they called his travel agent, and he told them where Harvey was. The Premier himself got into a helicopter and headed north.

By that time, Harvey had dropped to the ground and he was already in love with the place. He had always dreamed of a trapper's cabin where he could live by himself and write the Great Canadian Novel. Only liquor had kept him from his dreams. Now he asked Paul, "How far to the nearest wine store?"

"Two hundred miles," Paul said.

"Good."

Paul asked Harvey all the questions he had asked the Golden Boy, but Harvey wouldn't answer either. He claimed the Golden Boy had been stolen from the legislature by aliens.

"No," Paul said, "it's my vision. I can make it go away just by blinking."

"Then blink," Harvey said. "Make it disappear."

"Not till it answers a few questions," Paul replied. "It's a very stubborn vision. But it's the only one I've got." His words were nearly drowned out by the sound of the Premier's helicopter. The helicopter landed, and the Premier ran out to meet Paul.

"Thank God you've got the Golden Boy," the Premier said. "We must have it back."

"It's my vision," Paul said. "I could blink and make it disappear, but I need the answers to some questions."

"Perhaps I can help," the Premier said.

"Okay," Paul told him, "what does the future hold for me?"

"Great things," the Premier said.

"Why is the sky blue?"

"It's the light waves."

"Will I be able to go to law school and help my people?"

"I'll give you a scholarship myself."

"Who will win the Stanley Cup?"

"The Winnipeg Jets, of course."

"All right then," Paul said, and he blinked.

At that moment, in another universe, the captain of the Jovian starship B12 noticed that the onboard computer was off by two and a half degrees. He realized that the Golden Boy was not where it should be. He made a tricky adjustment and switched into warp mode. In a fraction of a second, he was two hundred miles northwest of Gillam. He clicked the transform responder switch twice and the Golden Boy reappeared on the top of the legislature.

The Premier gave Paul a ride home in his helicopter, Harvey began writing the Great Canadian Novel, and the Golden Boy looked down over the birthday celebrations. The captain of the starship circled the planet Perth, looking for the Golden Toy.

THE MAN WHO STOLE RECESS

nce on a sunny day in spring, a little girl named April woke up feeling very happy. She was in grade five and she liked school.

"The snow has finally gone," she told her mother. "And we're going to start skipping today. Melissa is going to bring her long skipping rope, and we're going to have turns. You can skip until you go out, and I'm going to keep my turn for the whole recess."

Her mother smiled and handed her her lunch.

That very same day, a boy in grade five named Albert was walking to school with his best friend Howie.

"If I keep my mouth shut until recess, and if Teacher doesn't ask me to go to the board, I think I'll make it." He'd had a hockey game the night before, and in the excitement of winning the community club title, he'd forgotten to do his homework. He was supposed to be doing a project on government grants and contracts.

Ms. Keystone, the teacher who taught grade five, told the secretary, "I don't have any breaks today, but I'll get the last of those reports done at recess so you can send them out."

The bell rang at nine o'clock, and all the kids and teachers rushed to their classrooms.

The principal walked up and down the hallway, looking in at the classes through the open doors and peeking through the little glass windows of the doors that were closed. He heard only the drone of teachers' voices and the skritch of chalk on the blackboard.

"This is good," he thought to himself. "This is the sound of education." He walked by an open door and heard a child laugh, but he was so pleased with his school that he didn't even go into the classroom and stop the child. Even the happy singing from the music room didn't bother him today.

Ten o'clock came. April whispered to Melissa, "Did you bring the rope?" Melissa nodded yes.

Ten-fifteen came. The teacher still hadn't called on Albert, so he dared to lift his eyes from his desk and look across the room. Howie grinned and gave him a high sign.

Ten twenty-five came and Ms. Keystone took the reports out of her second drawer and looked at them. All she had to do was sign them.

Ten-thirty came and every eye in the whole school was fixed on the clock. All the kids had closed their books. All the teachers were standing by the doors.

Nothing happened.

Ten thirty-six came. Melissa put the rope on her desk.

Still nothing.

At ten thirty-seven, Ms. Keystone said they might just as well look at last night's homework.

The whole class groaned. The first person called on was Albert.

"What about recess?" he said. "What happened to recess?" It seemed terribly unfair that recess had not come, and now he was going to be called upon.

"I don't know," Ms. Keystone said. "We didn't have any recess, did we? Maybe I should talk to the principal."

"I don't know what happened to recess," the principal said. "But it can't have gone far. It's always been around. I suppose it will be here this afternoon. Maybe it just forgot."

But recess didn't come that afternoon. And it didn't come all the next day or the next. Everybody was really worried, even the principal. When he walked down the hallways, he no longer heard the sounds of education. He heard a low rumbling grumble of protest like an animal that has been kept too long in a cave. The school was starting to get messy, and a lot of the children had stayed home with notes from their mothers.

Then on Friday, one of the grade six classes exploded. Later, nobody could quite remember what had happened. At ten thirty-two, all of the students suddenly stood up and tore their books in half. They ran around the classroom screaming. The teacher suddenly remembered that she had an appointment with her hairdresser and left. All of the kids just went home.

"This is impossible," the principal told Ms. Keystone. "We can't have students staying away and classrooms exploding. Someone will have to do something." Then he went into his office and locked the door. He unplugged his telephone so he wouldn't have to talk to any parents.

"All right, class," Ms. Keystone said. "Things have got into a terrible pickle. Does anyone have any idea what has become of recess?"

"Maybe it got run over," Howie suggested. "Maybe it ran out from behind a parked car and got run over on its way to school." Everybody agreed that if something that awful had happened, the police would have told them. Surely they would have known.

"Maybe it's sick," Melissa said. "Maybe it has tuberculosis and is locked away in quarantine in a hospital." But everybody agreed that the doctor would have sent a certificate if that had happened.

Finally, Herbert looked up from the physics book he was studying.

"Clayton has got recess," he said. "It was in all the newspapers." Herbert was too smart for his own good, and he always spent his time with his nose in a book, and he never even went out at recess, so nobody really knew him.

25

"Who is Clayton?" the whole class shouted at once.

"The Minister of Education," Herbert replied. "Or at least he is until the election. Then he's going to retire to his farm."

"But if he retires to his farm," somebody said, "what will happen to recess?"

"I suppose he'll put it out to pasture," Herbert said. "Or maybe he'll send it to the slaughterhouse. That's what happens to things that get old on a farm. Not that it matters. I never liked recess anyway."

The children were outraged, but Ms. Keystone managed to keep them away from Herbert.

"It's not his fault," she said. "He didn't steal recess. Clayton did."

"But what are we going to do?" the children asked.

"Nothing," Ms. Keystone said in a sad voice. "There's nothing we can do. The education minister can do whatever he wants and he doesn't have to consult kids."

On the way home after school that day, April, Melissa, Albert and Howie just happened to be walking together. They were all moaning "What can we do? What can we do?" when April suddenly had an idea.

"We'll rescue recess," she said. "We'll go out to the farm and rescue recess."

The next morning at seven o'clock they were ready. They had packed peanut butter sandwiches and apple juice for themselves and some green grass and a bottle of fresh air for recess, because they knew that recess liked the outdoors.

They waited at a bus stop until a bus that said Clayton's Farm came by. They climbed on board, and in no time they were at the farm. It was a beautiful farm in a gentle valley. There was nobody home but, though they looked high and low in all the barns and sheds, they couldn't find recess.

They were just leaving the farm in despair when Albert heard a faint sound.

"What was that?" he asked.

"What was what?" Melissa said.

"That noise," Albert replied. "That faint ringing noise."

The others sat and listened. At first they heard nothing. Then they heard the faint distant sound of bells that were warm and familiar and happy.

"Recess," they all shouted at the same time, and sure enough, there in a pigpen, hiding behind a trough, was recess. It looked tired and hungry and weak. The shed was full of pigs big enough to stomp poor recess to death.

"What are we going to do now?" Melissa asked.

"He'll never make it," Howie told her. "The pigs'll kill him."

But suddenly, Albert had an idea.

"My homework!" he shouted. "I brought my homework!" And he ran to the trough and threw in his papers full of information on government contracts and grants. In no time the pigs were at the trough in a frenzy of feeding, and April and Melissa managed to pull recess out of the pen and sneak him out the door. The children gave recess some green grass and some fresh air, and in no time, it was ringing as loud as ever. They played in the field by the pigpen for exactly fifteen minutes, then they gathered up recess in a special collecting bottle they had brought with them, and they took it back to school.

On Monday morning, at ten twenty-nine, all but four of the children in the school were glum and miserable. Ms. Keystone was sitting at her desk with her head in her hands. The principal was locked in his office.

Then at ten-thirty, the recess bell rang. Everybody sat up with stunned looks on their faces. Then they burst out the doors, into the fresh air and the green grass. They skipped, they threw baseballs, they ran and they turned somersaults. And after fifteen minutes, they went back to their classrooms. Ms. Keystone's chalk went skritch skritch on the blackboard, and the principal walked down the hallway smiling at the sound of education everywhere.

THE SILVER LINING

here was once a certain northern country that had chosen a foreign Queen as its head of state. It was a very democratic country, and its leaders, in their wisdom, had decided that though they very much admired royalty, it was much too expensive to keep your own when you could lease a perfectly good foreign royal family at a modest expense. Besides, having your own royal family was a dangerous business. There were always princesses being abducted by dragons or locked up in royal towers. Often the entire kingdom would be put to sleep for a hundred years until a prince got around to rousing a sleeping princess. That sort of thing played havoc with productivity, and trade suffered as a result.

No, the leaders decided, a parliament and a prime minister would have to do. Early in their history they had solved their yearning for royalty by getting a prime minister whose name was King, and though it wasn't really a satisfying solution, it was better than nothing. That prime minister discovered that the best way to run a northern country was by using a crystal ball and consulting the ghost of your dead mother or your dead dog. It was a young country and the Prime Minister tried to give it some dignity by collecting foreign ruins and erecting them in the capital.

Now, the people of the country had a habit of choosing prime ministers that they loved, but coming to despise them in very short order. So a certain prime minister who was recently elected after one of that country's periodical political purges decided that he would try to change the pattern and keep the people's love.

He consulted his crystal ball, of course. It is always kept perfectly polished on the prime ministerial desk. The Speaker of the House, a man of medium height, medium weight and medium intelligence, looked into the ball.

"What does it say?" the Prime Minister asked. "How can I get my people to love me?"

The Speaker looked into the crystal ball and spoke.

"Ruins," he said. "The people want ruins."

"I know they want ruins," the Prime Minister said. "But we can't afford ruins. I made a perfectly good bid on the Parthenon, but I was turned down by the Greek government. Egypt won't give up a single pyramid. The British are completely unreasonable on the question of Stonehenge. What am I to do?"

"You could consult the ghost of your beloved mother," the medium Speaker said.

"My mother," the Prime Minister told him, "is unfortunately alive. That won't work."

"Well, what about the ghost of your dog?"

"I never had a dog. Can't stand them."

"A cat?"

"No."

"A bird?"

"No. I once had a hamster named Cardinal Richelieu, but he unfortunately starved to death."

"Excellent," said the Speaker, and he covered his head with a towel and began to whisper to the crystal ball. At first Cardinal Richelieu was reluctant to speak to the Prime Minister. He apparently blamed the Prime Minister for forgetting to fill his

29

bowl, and so held him responsible for his premature demise. The Speaker spent most of his time trying to make people stop speaking, and so it was with some difficulty that he was able to convince the hamster to reply, but in the end he was successful. Cardinal Richelieu squeaked, "Hello, Jack."

"Hello," the Prime Minister said. "Sorry about the food."

"That's okay. Hamsters don't live very long anyway."

"My people want ruins," the Prime Minister said. "What can I do about that?"

"Give them ruins," Cardinal Richelieu said.

"Foreign ruins are too expensive," the Prime Minister protested. "Even with the GST we can't afford them."

"Make your own," the hamster squeaked. "That would be a good nationalistic gesture. And it would be cheap."

"But where am I to find the castles and churches to ruin?"

"Be innovative," the hamster said. "What are the most impressive Canadian buildings?"

"Hospitals," the Prime Minister said. "And universities."

"And what else?"

"Grain elevators."

"Good. What else?"

"Railways," the Prime Minister called out, warming to his task. "Airports. Publishing companies. Ballet and opera houses. The CBC. The West. The Maritimes."

"You've got it," Cardinal Richelieu said. "The people are going to love you."

And so the Prime Minister called his finance minister to come and visit him in the prime ministerial mansion.

"Paul," he said. "I have a great vision for this country. You are a man of great sophistication. You have travelled widely. What is it that makes our country different from the great countries of Europe?"

"I suppose their history," the Finance Minister said, for he had indeed travelled widely. "Their great cathedrals and monuments."

"And their ruins?"

"Yes, of course. The ruins."

"Paul," said the Prime Minister, "I am going to put you in charge of a great project. I am asking you to make this country greater than any of the countries of Europe. When you are through, I want our nation to have more ruins than any other nation on earth."

"What do you mean?" the Finance Minister cried in horror.

"I want you to find a way to turn some of our great hospitals and universities into ruins that will equal the Parthenon or the Roman baths at Trier," the Prime Minister said. "And the way to do it came to me this very moment," the Prime Minister went on. "I want you to cut transfer payment to the provinces. That way, they will be unable to operate their hospitals and universities, and in a very short time, the country will be filled with elegant ruins. Tourists will come from all over the world to see them."

"But if I do that, I'll ruin the social programs my father worked so hard to set up," the Finance Minister said. "He'd roll over in his grave."

"He could use the exercise," the Prime Minister said. "Besides, it's a small price to pay. And while you're at it could you cut funding to the arts and to publishing? Those guys have got some nice places we could make into dandy ruins."

"But I'll be a hated figure," the Finance Minister said. "Everyone will despise me."

"Look," the Prime Minister told him. "You were not very popular as a kid, were you?"

"Well, no."

"And nobody much liked you as an adult?"

"I had some friends."

"Yes, but not very many. That's why I chose you for Finance Minister. Everybody always hates the Finance Minister no matter what he does. So I didn't want to waste anybody who was popular. The people already hate you, even though you haven't brought down your first budget. Do what I say, and you won't be popular, but you'll be respected. It's better than nothing."

"You are a wise man," the Finance Minister said. "I only

hope that when I am Prime Minister, I will be as wise as you."
And he left to do the Prime Minister's bidding.

The Prime Minister called in his Minister of Human Resources.

"Lloyd," he said. "I want to make this country as great as any in Europe." And he explained his theory about the ruins.

"I'm sorry," the Human Resources Minister said, "but I'm not in charge of very many buildings."

"Next to the ruins," the Prime Minister said, "what is the thing you notice most about the great nations of the world?"

"Their cafés, I suppose," the Human Resources Minister answered. "People sipping wine at tables with umbrellas. People walking in parks and along riverbanks. People having picnics in remote mountain valleys. All the things that go with leisure."

"Precisely," the Prime Minister said. "And I want our people to have that kind of leisure. I know you have embarked on great projects to create jobs, but you know what more jobs mean, don't you?"

"More work?"

"Less leisure," the Prime Minister said with a grin that went from ear to ear. "Now I want you to abandon all projects that create jobs."

"But then we will have more people on unemployment insurance," the Minister said.

"Pay attention," the Prime Minister said. "I told you I want more leisure. I want you to cut unemployment insurance so that people don't have to stand in line to get benefits and they can spend more time with their families. And while you're at it you may as well cut aid to day-cares so that mothers and fathers can spend more time with their children."

"You are a wise man," the Minister of Human Resources said. "I only hope that when I am Prime Minister, I will be equally wise." And he left to do the Prime Minister's bidding.

The Prime Minister's day was very busy. He called in the Minister of Heritage, who agreed to cut funding to the CBC so that its stunning new building would soon be in ruins. He called in the Minister of Agriculture and the Minister of Transport, who agreed that the Crow Rate should be cut so that the grain elevators of the West could become the magnificent ruins for which they had always seemed destined.

"I don't think them Crows should have been hauling grain anyway," the Prime Minister said, and his ministers murmured their agreement. He asked the Transport Minister to guarantee that the railways would cease operations so that their great bridges and railway yards would be available for tourists who wished to take photographs, but it turned out that the previous government had already closed most of the tracks and had begun the heavy job of turning airports into mausoleums.

Then he called his entire cabinet together for a meeting.

"Ladies and gentlemen," he said, "I have begun a brave new program for this country. The polls already show that I am the most popular prime minister in decades. Now I want to share my good fortune with you. I want you to take all the credit for these great new undertakings. I will sit humbly in the background, and claim no credit at all."

The ministers wept for joy and kissed the Prime Minister's hand. They all thanked him profusely. Only one minister held back, the Minister of Justice.

"When all these wonderful programs begin to take effect," he murmured to himself, "the people of this country may not be as pleased as they are at the moment. I believe I'll pass a series of laws to create tighter gun control. That will make it a good deal safer to be a member of the government."

Rome wasn't built in a day. It's been a while now since the policies were passed, and the country still hasn't caught up with Europe. Everybody admits that there is a great deal more leisure now that fewer people are working, and the Japanese have lately been organizing tours of empty universities and hospitals without beds. The elevators are crumbling on schedule, the opera and ballet houses are magnificent in their emptiness, and the silence of the national airwaves is truly impressive. All in all, the Prime Minister has every reason to feel optimistic.

FROGMARCH

he land of Nord was peculiarly blessed. Though the inhabitants would have readily confessed that in winter it was hardly more than a few acres of snow, in summer it was spectacular. It had almost any kind of landscape you could wish for: mountains and prairies and lakes and rivers and seacoasts. And even in winter, if you dressed warmly, there were sixteen different kinds of snow you could enjoy. You could ski over it, or walk through it, or catch it on the end of your tongue as you walked through pine forests.

One warm, fall day in the land of Nord, a sparrow and a frog chanced to meet near a pond. The sparrow settled in the lowest branch of a willow tree, and the frog leaned back on his lily pad.

"It's certainly beautiful here," said the sparrow.

"This is frog country," said the frog. "It's been frog country since the beginning of time. In this part of Nord, everyone speaks Frog. Chugarum."

The sparrow hesitated, but he did want to talk to the frog, so he said in his small sparrow voice, "Chugarum."

"Not bad," said the frog. "Not bad at all. But try to get a rising inflection at the end. Chugarum."

"Chugarum," said the sparrow.

"I don't suppose you'll ever get it right, Old Chap," said the frog, "but it's good to see you try."

"You speak excellent Sparrow," the sparrow said to the frog. "Where did you learn to speak such excellent Sparrow?"

"Well," the frog replied, "I did study at the London School of Fogonomics. It was a jolly good time too."

"You know," the sparrow said, "I was thinking of setting up a small business here in the big Pond. I was thinking of setting up a small restaurant selling Welsh rarebit."

"I don't think it would go over all that well," the frog said. "Mosquitoes, yes. Flies, yes, even the odd moth or butterfly, but you'll find that frogs don't eat a lot of rabbits. Far too large and furry for our taste."

"Well," said the sparrow, "I wasn't thinking of real rabbits. Welsh rarebit is sort of like a piece of toast with cheese melted over it."

"Ah, well, that's a different thing," said the frog. "Frogs like a bit of cheese now and then. Do you know that in the mother-pond there are over three hundred different kinds of cheese?"

"I've heard that," said the sparrow, "although I wasn't actually thinking of marketing especially to frogs. I was thinking rather of the bird market. There are a lot of different birds who live around the Pond. Ducks and geese and snipes and gulls and terns. I was thinking of hanging out a sign saying Sparrow's Old-Fashioned Welsh Rarebit."

"Can't be done," said the frog. "In this part of Nord, all signs must be in Frog. You can make your menu in both Frog and Sparrow if you like, but the outside sign must be in Frog."

"And what is Frog for Sparrow's Old-Fashioned Welsh Rarebit?" asked the sparrow.

"Chugarum," said the frog.

"I beg your pardon," the sparrow said.

"Chugarum. That's Frog for Sparrow's Old-Fashioned Welsh Rarebit."

"Suppose I were to call it simply The Old Country Rarebit Inn."

"Ah," said the frog. "That would be Chugarum."

"But that's the same word!"

"No. No. It's all a matter of pronunciation. Not *chugarum,* but *chugarum.*"

"I see," said the sparrow.

Just then, a duck and a gull walked by. "Chugarum," they said in unison.

The frog answered, "Chugarum."

"What did they say?" the sparrow asked.

"The duck said it was a very fine day. The gull asked after my aging mother. I told them it has been the finest summer in years and reminded them to vote in the referendum on Monday."

"But all any of you said was 'chugarum.' "

"It's a question of accent," the frog said. "It's not what you say, but how you say it."

"And what is this referendum about?" the sparrow asked.

The frog was about to answer when another frog hopped over from a neighbouring pad. He limped slightly and carried a silver cane. There was barely enough room for the two of them on the lily pad.

The sparrow was about to ask a question when the first frog silenced him.

"Hush," he said. "Don't ask him about the cane. It's a delicate question. It happened at a restaurant. He went into the kitchen to congratulate the chef on a particularly fine meal, and the chef mistook him for . . . well . . . let's just say it was an unfortunate misunderstanding."

"I suppose he said 'chugarum' and the chef answered, chugarum, and then . . ."

"Precisely," the frog said. "You are a sparrow of the world. You understand these things. But please be careful not to offend him. He is the most important frog on the block."

"Chugarum," said the second frog.

"Chugarum," the sparrow answered. "But would you mind if we spoke Sparrow? Frog is such a difficult language."

"Indeed it is," said the second frog. "That is its beauty. Frog is a language of endless nuance."

"Could you tell me about your referendum?" the sparrow asked. "I am thinking of setting up a business here at the Pond, but there are rumours from elsewhere in the land of Nord that it might be dangerous to do so until the referendum has been held."

"Pay no attention to the rumours," the second frog said. "We are voting to declare the Pond a separate nation, but nothing will change."

"But surely if you separate from Nord, then you will have to at least negotiate borders."

"No," the second frog said, "the borders will remain the same."

"But what about the currency?" the sparrow asked. "If I am to invest in the Pond then I have only Nord dollars to invest."

"Rest assured," the first frog said, "we shall continue to use the currency of Nord."

"Then there is the question of trade," the sparrow said. "In order to make my Welsh rarebits I must buy bread from Philadelphia, which is the only place in North America that makes authentic Welsh bread, and cheese from Frontario and salt from the salt mines of Susquatchewan. Though mine is a small business, it has both national and international connections."

"Fear not," the second frog told the sparrow. "All trade connections will remain the same. We shall still be favoured among the provinces of Nord so that you may trade freely with Frontario and we will retain membership in the Northern International Free Trade Yoke, or NIFTY, as it is called."

"I travel a lot," the sparrow began, but before he could finish, the first frog interrupted him and said, "You will even be able to continue to use your Nord passport."

"Then what will have changed?" the sparrow asked. "Why are you having your referendum at all?"

"Everything will have changed," said the first frog. "I will be the president of a free sovereign nation. I will be able to travel to other countries and sign my name on documents."

"We will have our pride," said the second frog. "Pride justifies every kind of risk."

Suddenly, a third frog jumped onto the lily pad, very nearly sinking it in the process. He was a very big frog, but very young. The sparrow recognized him as a mountain frog, while the other two were swamp frogs.

"Pay no attention to them," he told the sparrow. "I represent the youth of the Pond, and as soon as the referendum is over and the *yes* vote has passed, everything will change. We will have no connection at all with the country of Nord, which has sorely oppressed us since time immemorial, except, of course, for the usual economic connections. One of our first acts will be to close down your Welsh rarebit restaurant and replace it with one that sells only mosquitoes and flies."

"But then all the birds will flee from the Pond," the sparrow said.

"Precisely," the big young frog answered. "There will be no room for birds in the new Pond. For too long the great blue herons and the terns from the mountain have preyed on innocent young frogs, preventing them from achieving their destinies."

"Pay no attention to him," the first frog said. "He is merely young and impulsive."

"He will learn the exigencies of power once we are sovereign," said the second frog.

"Just you wait for the referendum," the big young mountain frog growled.

"Are you all agreed on the referendum?" the sparrow asked.

"Oh, yes," the frogs all answered together.

"Exactly."

"Jolly good."

"Chugarum."

"And what precisely does the referendum ask?" the sparrow said. "It must have been very difficult to get the exact wording."

"Why, not at all," said the first frog. "The question is 'chugarum?'"

"And of course the voters have a choice," said the second frog. "They may answer 'chugarum.'"

"Or even 'chugarum,'" said the big young frog, "though of course we do not expect that."

"And after the vote, everything will be different?" the sparrow asked. The lily pad was beginning to sink under the weight of the frogs.

"Yes, yes," the frogs agreed. "Everything will be different."

"And everything will be the same?" the sparrow went on.

"Oh, yes," the frogs said. "Everything will be exactly the same.

And it came to pass that the referendum was held, and just as everyone feared and expected, the answer was "chugarum." And since then, everything has been quite different but just the same as before.

The Land of Plenty

nce upon a time there was a perfect little country named Frontario. It had mountains and rivers and plains in just the right proportion. It had long lazy summers and cold hardy winters, and the animals of Frontario were happy. The lion did not lie down with the lamb, because the lamb was not a stupid animal, but the squirrels collected just enough acorns to get them through the winter, and the wolves, though they hunted, ate no more than they needed. In Frontario, the needy were cared for and the sick were cured.

Then one day, two small mice were talking together.

"Just imagine," said the first mouse, "a pile of grass seeds higher than that oak over there. So much grass seed that it would take a thousand years to eat it all. Enough grass seed to take care of you and your family until the end of time."

"I could never eat that much grass seed," said the second mouse. "The rain and the wind and the snow would spoil it long before winter was over."

"Not if you built a gigantic granary," said the first mouse. "Then it would last forever."

"But if I had so much grass seed," the second mouse replied, "then the other mice would come and take it away."

"Not if you had laws to keep them from taking your property. Not if you had a police force and an army to stop them."

"I have all I need now," said the second mouse. "And so do you."

"Yes, I know," sighed the first mouse. "Everyone knows this is the best country in the world to live. But sometimes I like to dream about being rich, even if it will never happen."

At the very same moment, two frogs lazed on a lily pad in the sun.

The first frog said, "Have you ever considered how wonderful it would be if the Pond were not just a small pond but a giant lake that covered plains and forests and mountains, and the lake was covered with lily pads and the flies were so thick that you needed only to flick out your tongue to catch one?"

"It might be interesting," said the second frog. "But then there would be a lot more frogs and a lot fewer other animals. What would happen to the other animals, the mice and the gophers and the squirrels and the cows and the horses and the sheep?"

"That would be their problem," said the first frog.

"Yes," said the second frog. "But the world is more interesting when it is filled with a range of animals. Frogs are important, but so are other animals. We should all share the good things of the world."

"I guess you are right," sighed the first frog. "But sometimes I like to imagine a world dominated by frogs, where only the things that frogs cared about mattered, and we could forget about all the other animals. I know that will never happen, but I like to dream about it."

As the mice dreamed in the meadow and the frogs dreamed on the lily pad, a couple of eagles circled in the sky overhead.

"We are the luckiest creatures in the world," said the first eagle. "The fish in the ocean eat plankton and grubs and turn them into their own flesh. The mice and the gophers eat seeds and plants and turn them into their own flesh. The small birds in the trees and the frogs in the ponds eat insects and spiders and turn them into their own flesh. Then we eat the fish and the gophers and the mice and the small birds. We are at the very top of the food chain. We eat everything else, but nothing eats us."

"And yet," said the second eagle, "I sometimes feel strangely dissatisfied. There are hundreds and thousands of birds and animals that never provide a meal for an eagle. They pass their days in idleness, collecting seeds or insects or grubs, eating or mating or just sleeping in the sun. From an eagle's point of view, they are useless, mere parasites using up resources that could be used for eagle-enhancing things."

"I see your point," said the first eagle. "But we must take into account the special luck that has made us eagles rather than mere sparrows. *Noblesse oblige*. We have a duty to those who are weaker and less fortunate than we."

"Perhaps you are right," said the second eagle. "It is what our fathers and mothers taught us, but perhaps also you are wrong. It may be that a world run entirely for the benefit of eagles would be the best of all possible worlds. Perhaps we need only to dare to dream."

Now it happened that Frontario had always been governed either by the Reds or the Blues or the Oranges. Each party claimed that it best represented the wishes of the people, and that it could govern with the greatest efficiency and the greatest kindness. When the Reds were in power, they built roads and hospitals and schools, and said the world was changing for the better. When the Blues were in charge, they built roads and hospitals and schools and said that they were maintaining the traditional values of the country. When the Oranges were in power, they built roads and hospitals and schools and said that they were radically altering the nature of the country to make it more fair.

All of the animals belonged to one of the three parties. It is true that most mice belonged to the Orange party and most eagles belonged to the Blue party, but when they voted in elections, both mice and eagles expected that nothing very much was going to change.

Now there was a fourth party, the United Ogres, who met under bridges and discussed the ways in which they could dismantle the highways and close down the hospitals and shut all the schools. They were never elected and in fact seldom took part in elections. Most of them ran radio talk shows or operated small, poor farms.

One day, three of the ogres chanced to meet under a bridge.

"It's an unnatural world," the first ogre said.

"Nature red in tooth and claw," replied the second. That's the usual greeting and response when ogres chance to meet. Ogres hate anything that relies on cooperation. They believe in pure competitiveness. They think that in a world of pure survival of the fittest, ogres would fare much better than the other animals because they are stronger and meaner.

"There are simply not enough of us," the third ogre said. "We will never win an election so that we can make this a better world for ogres."

"Sad but true," replied the second.

Suddenly a dark form appeared from behind the pilings of the bridge. It was the troll who lived there, and trolls are so evil that even ogres are afraid of them.

"Dark dreams," the troll said. "Believe in yourselves. Put your faith in dark dreams, and you'll win." And he disappeared behind the dark pilings.

"What did he mean?" asked the second ogre.

"I think I know," said the first ogre. "He spoke of being ourselves and dark dreams. To be an ogre is to dream dark dreams. We are the only creatures honest enough to speak of our dark dreams, and when we do, we are shunned by the others. We must become like the others and make them acknowledge their dark dreams. We must make them believe that their darkest dreams are common sense."

Because for centuries ogres have been feared and hunted by the other animals, they have learned to be shape changers.

Now each of the ogres took on the shape of a chameleon. The first ogre joined the Blue party, the second ogre joined the Red party, and the third ogre joined the Orange party. They said all the right things, and in no time at all they came to lead their parties.

When the election was called, all of the parties promised roads and hospitals and schools. In this particular election, the Blue party won, but it might have been the Red or even the Orange. What happened was that the ogre went to the mice and said, "Wouldn't the world be better if we drained the ponds so that there would be more grass seed for mice?"

The mice said it was a pity about the frogs, but times were tough, and they voted for the ogre. The ogre then went to the frogs and said, "Wouldn't the world be better if we flooded all the grassland so there would be more space for frogs?"

The frogs said it was a pity about the mice, but times were tough, and they voted for the ogre.

Then the ogre went to the eagles and said, "Wouldn't it be a better world if all the animals that lazed all day and merely fed and mated and did nothing to further the cause of eagles were exterminated?"

The eagles sighed and said *noblesse oblige,* and voted for the ogre. And of course he won the election.

The day after the election, the ogre took off his costume and revealed that he was an ogre.

"Nothing has changed," the animals said. "We have simply voted for an ogre. He will have to give us roads and hospitals and schools."

But the ogre did not give them roads. He closed the hospitals and he shut down the schools. He flooded the grasslands and he drained the ponds. He put an end to the creatures who only fed and mated and did nothing for the good of eagles. And when some of the animals came to him to complain, he merely said, "Dream your darkest dreams." And they voted for him again. And they dreamt dark dreams. And as far as anyone knows, they are dreaming them still.

THE BIRTHDAY PARTY

he animals of the forest were not much given to talking. Oh, the wolves howled at night, the squirrels chattered in the trees and the birds sang, but it was rare that any of them actually talked. And that's not surprising, because nobody talked to them. Sometimes the farmer cursed at the gophers who were digging holes in his field, and sometimes he cursed the blackbirds who ate his oats, but the things he said were not very nice, and the blackbirds and the gophers never bothered to answer.

So of course it was a real surprise when a little girl named Shannon walked into the middle of the forest and went right up to a frog who was minding his own business by the edge of the pool and said, "It's our birthday."

"Not mine," said the frog. "My birthday is not for another month." Then he realized what he'd done and said, "Chugarum."

The frog had once been a prince who had to spend all his time attending horrible boring state dinners, but a very nice witch had taken pity on him and turned him into a frog, and now he had nothing to do all day but lie around on a lily pad and sleep. She'd warned him that if he weren't careful, a beautiful young maiden might kiss him and turn him back into a prince, and then he'd have to go back and listen to politicians talking all day. He didn't want that to happen, so he said "chugarum" once more so that Shannon wouldn't know he was a prince.

"We have to have a party," Shannon said, paying no attention to the chugarums. "And I'm going to need your help inviting all the animals."

"Okay," the frog said. "But only if you promise that you won't kiss me."

"You are a very nice-looking frog," Shannon said, "as far as frogs go. But you have to admit that you are cold and green and quite slimy. No offence, but I really don't have any desire to kiss you."

"Good," said the frog.

"And I wish you'd stop saying 'chugarum,'" Shannon told him. "I don't think it's a very nice word. In fact, I believe it's a swear word in Polish."

"It's a perfectly good word in Frog," the frog replied. "It means both hello and goodbye at the same time. You use it when you'd just as soon not talk to someone. But we could ask the turtle."

"The turtle?"

"Yes," the frog said. "Turtles speak Polish."

"I thought they would have spoken Turtle," Shannon said.

"Of course they speak Turtle," the frog said. "But their second language is Polish. Just like the deer who speak Ukrainian and the squirrels who speak Spanish and the seagulls who speak Icelandic."

"Do all the animals speak different languages?" Shannon asked.

"Of course," the frog said. "This is a multicultural forest. The English sparrow only speaks English, but all the other animals are bilingual, or in the case of birds, bisongual."

"I've never heard of the word *bisongual*," Shannon said.

"I suppose there are a great number of things you have not heard of," the frog said. "You are, after all, a very young girl."

"Not so young," Shannon said. "I'm seven. But what I came to tell you is that altogether, we are a hundred and twenty-five. It's our hundred and twenty-fifth birthday."

"Let's see," said the frog. "You're seven. And I'm three, which is twenty-one in frog years. So that makes twenty-eight. And the goldfinches in that flock are each two, and there are forty of them so that's eighty, for a total of a hundred and eight. And there are a million mosquitoes, each of them a half year old. So that makes five hundred thousand, one hundred and eight. And we haven't even counted the foxes and the pheasants and the fish. I'll bet that altogether, we're over a million years old."

"You're just being silly," Shannon told the frog. "The rocks are many millions of years old. But I'm talking about the province. Manitoba is a hundred and twenty-five years old today."

"Well then. Let's have a party," the frog said.

"That's what I told you," Shannon said. "We have to hold a party and invite everybody."

"Maybe not everybody," the frog said. "There are a lot of mosquitoes and blackflies in Manitoba. We might not have enough cake to go around, and then they'd start to eat the other guests."

Shannon thought for a moment. "They can send a delegation. And so can all the squishy things like worms and grubs, and of course the snakes. Snakes are all green and slimy."

"I don't think that should disqualify them," the frog said. "A little bit of green slime never hurt anyone. In fact, it makes for rather a pretty coat when the sun shines on it."

Shannon realized that she had hurt the frog's feelings. "It's not so much the green slime," she said. "But they do have a habit of eating things, you know, mice and gophers and frogs."

"Frogs?" the frog shouted in dismay. "You mean snakes eat frogs? Well, then they should certainly be disqualified. That's disgusting."

47

"We'll just ask a few garter snakes," Shannon said. "They only eat insects."

"As long as they don't eat too many," the frog grumbled. "There are hardly enough to go around as it is."

"Where shall we hold the party?" Shannon asked the frog.

"Right here," the frog said. "We've got lots of lakes and ponds and rivers and fields and forests and even some hills."

"Where did you get the hills?" Shannon asked. "I didn't know there were any hills in Manitoba."

"They're in the west," the frog said. "They're not exactly mountains, but we're not inviting any mountain lions anyway."

"We'll send out invitations," Shannon said. "I've brought a box of crayons. You can have the blue ones and the black ones, and I'll use the red ones and the yellow ones."

"And you can write the ones in Hindi and Sanskrit and Urdu for the geese and the fish and the rabbits. And I'll write the ones in French and English and Italian for the swans and the sparrows and the caribou. If we each do half a million, we'll be finished in no time."

"It's no use," Shannon said. "I can't speak any of those languages."

"And neither can I," said the frog. "So there we are."

"It's very sad," Shannon said. "It's Manitoba's hundred and twenty-fifth birthday party. And no one will come because we can't make the invitations."

"I know," the frog said. "We'll ask the goat. He used to be a member of the Manitoba Court of Appeals before he retired. He'll know what to do."

The goat had a long white beard, and he spoke with a Scottish accent.

"If you didn't want anybody to know about the party, what would you do?" the goat asked.

"I'd say it was secret," Shannon said.

"But what if you told a gossip?" the goat asked.

"Then pretty soon everyone would know."

"Exactly," the goat said, and he started to munch a tin can.

Then Shannon and the frog went down to the pond and

they found a goose. Now, everybody knows that a goose can't keep a secret.

"Don't tell anyone," Shannon said to the goose, "because it's a secret. But we're holding a one hundred and twenty-fifth birthday party for Manitoba right here on July 15th. Remember. Don't tell a soul."

But the goose told a duck and the duck told a chipmunk and the chipmunk told a skunk, and in no time at all, every creature in the province knew about the party. And when the day came, they were all there, even the mosquitoes and the blackflies, but everybody agreed that it wouldn't really have been a Manitoba party without a few biting insects. Shannon was so happy that she nearly kissed the frog, but he saw her coming and jumped into the pond, and they all lived happily ever after.

IF PIGS COULD FLY

nce upon a time there were three little Pigs, a
Red Pig, an Orange Pig and a Blue Pig. They lived
in a pen in the middle of Jean's barn, and since
they had never left the barn, they believed that
the barn was the whole world, and they were
the centre of the world. They were pretty much the same size,
but each one wanted to be the biggest.

One day Farmer Jean came into the barn and said, "You
are the smartest animals on the farm. I am getting tired, and I
need someone to run the farm for me. Whichever of you puts
on the most weight by April 25 will be declared the winner,
and will be put in charge of all the animals on the farm. But I
am not going to give you any more food. In fact, my accountant, Mr. Martin, has asked me to reduce the amount of food
for all the animals. Good luck."

The Blue Pig was the first to respond. "I am certain to win,"
he told the others. "I am already the largest. I am pretty much
in charge around here right now. I'd suggest that you guys give
me your food and forget about the contest."

"Oh, no," the Red Pig said. "I have been expecting just such a contest, and a poll of all the animals on the farm suggests that I am nearly as large as you. I have consulted with many of the other animals, and they are prepared to give me portions of their food. By the 25th of April, I will be the largest Pig."

"Not so fast," the Orange Pig grunted. "I have lost some weight, it is true, but I have been the largest Pig in the past, and I will be the largest Pig again."

Then the three Pigs travelled around the barn, consulting the other animals. They all agreed that they would offer a Brave New World, though they disagreed about the best way to achieve it.

The Blue Pig went straight to the little Blue Hen.

"What is your advice?" he asked her.

"Well," she said, "all the animals are concerned about security. I am sure they would give you some of their food if you were to stand up for Law and Order."

"I'm certainly in favour of Law and Order," the Blue Pig told the little Blue Hen. "But what should I promise the animals?"

"You know the Old Woman Who Lives in a Shoe? Well, I believe she's been cheating on welfare. I'd recommend that you take her off the welfare rolls. And she has so many children that she doesn't know what to do with them. I'd suggest you take them out of the shoe and put them in Boot Camp."

"An excellent idea," the Blue Pig said, and he ran off to write a press release that very minute.

The Red Pig went to consult his friend the Horse.

"Education," the Horse said. "A little bit of Horse sense, that's the answer. Educate the animals, and they'll give you their food."

"What a wonderful idea," the Red Pig said, and he went out knocking on the stall doors, trying to get all the animals who taught other animals to help him.

The Orange Pig went to his friend Bossy the Cow.

"What should I promise the other animals?" he asked.

"Health," she said. "The milk of human kindness. The animals are all afraid that Farmer Jean is going to cut back on the budget for health so that all the veterinarians will go south to the land of Milk and Honey. Promise them Health."

"What a good idea," the Orange Pig said, and he called a press conference to release his pamphlet on Health Reform. "The Red Pig has been squandering food," he said. "If I become the biggest Pig, I will reallocate those resources to Health, keeping some in reserve in case Jean's accountant Martin cuts back even further."

The next day, the polls showed that it was nip and tuck. No Pig had a decided advantage.

The Blue Pig consulted his friend the Fox. "Balance your budget," the Fox told him.

"What a wonderful idea," the Blue Pig said. "But how will I do that?"

"The Mice are inveterate gamblers," the Fox said. "If you put a Video Lottery Terminal into every Mouse hole, you will have enough grain to balance the budget and make you the fattest Pig in the country."

"What a wonderful idea," the Blue Pig said. And he made up a pamphlet and had it delivered to every pen in the barn.

The Red Pig went to the Hen house and conducted a poll. Most of the Hens were in favour of abortion on demand. The Red Pig announced, "I am in favour of Abortion." Then his friends gathered around him and told him that he was not actually in favour of Abortion. "I am not in favour of Abortion," he announced.

The Orange Pig consulted a Beaver who was visiting from the Farm across the Pond. "Jobs," the Beaver told him. "Everybody wants to work. Everyone wants to keep busy."

"What a good idea," the Orange Pig said, and he wrote *Jobs* in his book.

The Blue Pig saw that the Orange Pig had a book full of promises, so he got himself a book too. He wrote in it. "We must get out of Debt. We will not spend any money for a very long time." And he was so satisfied with himself that he left the book in plain view in the stall, and went to sleep.

The Red Pig was upset. "The Orange Pig has a book," he

said. "And so does the Blue Pig." So he went out and bought himself a book.

"Alas," he said, "there is nothing in this book." Then he noticed that the Blue Pig and the Orange Pig were sleeping, and had left their books unattended. So he took a page from the Blue Pig's book that said Education, and he photocopied it. Then he took the page from the Orange Pig's book that said Health, and he photocopied that too. Then he pasted the pages into his own book. "There," he said. "Now I too have a book that I can consult if I wish to know what I believe."

The next day the Blue Pig gathered his friends around him. "All your friends are in the south half of the barn," a Praying Mantis told him. "Promise to help the south side of the barn." And so he did.

The Orange Pig's friends gathered together to advise him. "All your friends are in the north half of the barn," the Cat said. "Promise to help the north." And so he did.

The Red Pig's friends could not suggest a direction for the Red Pig. The Dog said, "Tell the animals that you are a personal friend of Farmer Jean, and that if you become biggest Pig, you will be able to count on his generosity." And so he did.

Things went on in this way for quite a long time. Then one day the roof of the barn sprang a leak. In no time there was a large puddle in the middle of the Pig pen. The three Pigs looked into the puddle and realized that they had been working so hard to win the contest that they had forgotten to eat. They were all much thinner than they had been the day the contest had begun. They realized then, although making promises was very enjoyable, it was not enough to sustain them. So they all ran to the trough and began to eat as much as they could.

And if I'm not mistaken, they are still there.

PUDDLE AND POND

 nce upon a time, the animals of Small Puddle on Farmer Jean's farm were gathered out near the old oak. It was a sunny day, the birds were twittering in the treetops, and the flowers bowed their heads in the gentle breeze. Big Frog was the first to speak.

"It's a whole new ball game," he said. "International trade is where it's at. We've got to diversify, make the things we make best and trade with the other ponds. Otherwise, we've had it. It's a dog-eat-dog world out there."

"I assume that's a figure of speech," Rover said. He was a fairly large sheepdog, but in spite of his size, he was sensitive. "I hope you were not making reference to a stereotypical myth about canine cannibalism."

"I'm sorry," Big Frog said. He wasn't really very sorry, and he often complained to his wife that in these days of political correctness you could hardly say anything at all, but he did want to get re-elected and he couldn't afford to alienate potential voters.

"Besides, what we make best," said a small mouse who had

just poked his head out from under a pile of straw, "is grass and flowers and trees and honey." He ducked his head back under the straw as the shadow of a hawk from Big Pond to the south swept by.

"That's just the kind of small thinking that keeps you a mouse," Big Frog said. "Lack of initiative and narrow provincialism are going to doom us to a minor role in the affairs of the farm unless we make wholesale changes. There's a market for our grasses providing hay for the cattle market. Florist's shops around the world need flowers. Our trees can be sold as lumber and our honey converted to sugar." Big Frog smiled at his own cleverness, and waited for a reply.

"I had hoped to stay a mouse," the mouse replied. "I know that a mouse is only a small weak creature, but we are peaceful. We don't start wars. We mind our own business. We search for grains and sometimes we have good years and sometimes bad years, but on the whole, being a mouse is not such a bad thing." The mouse was not accustomed to making such long speeches, and he had forgotten to watch the sky. He saw the shadow at the last moment and dived for cover. The hawk missed him, though it did carry off a part of his tail.

"As to the cattle trade," said Bossy, a Jersey cow who had been quietly chewing her cud, "the less said about that disgusting and murderous business, the better. I hope we are not going to sink so low as to engage in that sort of thing."

"Honey," said a passing bumblebee, "is food for baby bees. It is not a proper item for trade."

"You people have no imagination," Big Frog said in disgust. "It is no longer enough just to be a mouse or a cow or even a frog. We have to think big."

"I suppose if I were an elephant," the mouse said, "then that hawk would leave me alone. But once at a conference I attended, I slept next to an elephant, and it was a very uncomfortable experience. It tossed and turned all night and I didn't get a wink of sleep."

"A conference!" cried Big Frog. "What a wonderful idea. Why don't I invite all the biggest ponds on the farm to send

55

their leaders to a conference here at Small Puddle? That will turn the whole farm's attention to us. I think I will call it the Great Big Seven conference. There will be representatives from the six biggest ponds and us."

"Perhaps I can help put some perspective on this issue," said the mallard. He had flown all over the farm, and he even spent his winters in the south, so many of the animals paid attention to what he said. "There are a great many ponds on the farm, even more than the six you have mentioned. We are merely a puddle, and not even the largest puddle at that."

"All the more reason that we should seize the initiative," Big Frog said. "Things have changed. We've got to get out there and aggressively pursue new markets, otherwise we'll stay a backwater."

"A backwater is not so bad," a shiner piped up from the edge of the puddle. "Big fish eat little fish, and if you're a little fish then a backwater is just where you want to be." At that very moment, a tern dropped from the sky and swallowed the shiner.

"Sorry," the tern said. "I hope I didn't interrupt anything?"

"No, no," Big Frog answered. "We were pretty much finished with our conversation anyway."

And so Big Frog set up the conference for the Great Big Seven. At first he was worried that the others wouldn't accept his invitation, but they all agreed to come. Everybody at Small Puddle agreed that Big Frog had done a fine thing. They had never seen such big and ferocious-looking animals as those that came from the other six ponds.

The eagle from the south was the first to comment. "You have among the finest-looking gophers I have ever seen," he said. "Your mice are plump and sleek and many of your small birds seem almost delectable. I am sure we will be able to make a trade to our mutual advantage."

And so Big Frog sneaked out of the building and held a referendum to determine whether the citizens of Small Puddle would trade gophers and mice and small birds for important new items of software. Everybody voted for this new trade initiative except for certain gophers and mice and small birds, but everyone agreed that they simply lacked vision.

Then the Emperor Bird from the Pond of the Rising Sun said, "You have some lovely beef and lumber that we would be willing trade for certain items of hardware."

Even Bossy the cow voted in favour, because she didn't understand that "beef" meant "cow meat." She thought it was something French. The only ones to complain were certain birds and animals that lived in trees, but Big Frog told them about the future of plastics, and in the next opinion poll, he was even more popular than he had been before.

Then the hawk from the Gallic Pond to the east said, "Nous aimons vos chevaux. We very much admire your 'orses. They are, what you say, un culinary delight."

The stallions of Small Puddle were reluctant to agree until Big Frog explained to them that the Culinary Delight was a famous horse race in France. The stallions loved to race, and they stamped their feet and whinnied in approval. The hawk went on to compliment Big Frog on his elegant legs, and Big Frog was pleased. He had always prided himself on his legs, but no one had actually offered him a compliment before.

"We must do lunch one day," the hawk said.

"I'd be delighted," Big Frog said, and he thought to himself how much he and the hawk had in common, what with their shared interest in frogs' legs.

"Ach du Lieber," exclaimed the stork from the Pond of the Huns of the North. "I have heard of the delicious fish from Small Puddle, and we would be willing to trade certain items of miraculous engineering for such fish." Unfortunately, a Spanish tern had eaten the very last shiner in Small Puddle only a very short time before, and no trade was possible.

"Well, perhaps you would allow us to do some military training in your wilderness, drop a few minor bombs in un-important places in return for which we will share our military technology with you." That seemed a particularly good deal, and everyone voted for it.

Then the lion from the Island of the Shared Queen in the

Channel Pond roared out, "Mutton and wool. I must have mutton and wool. In return for which we will send scholars from our mightiest universities to teach you how to stammer so that you will seem as beautiful as we."

The sheep were divided about the advantages of the deal. None of them liked the idea of mutton, and they were even more upset at the idea of lamb chops. The winters at Small Puddle could be very cold, and they did not much like the idea of doing without their coats. But Big Frog took one of them aside and told him how much warmer fibreglass insulation was than wool. That sheep voted in favour of the trade, and the rest of the sheep, because they were sheep after all, voted with him.

Finally a bear from the Big Siberian Pond, who had not actually been invited but who had come as an observer said, "We have nothing to trade with you because until lately we were a Communist pond. But we are now engaged in Free Enterprise. We are desperately in need of seeds and grains and berries. We can only offer you some very clever criminals in the short run, but once we are fully capitalist, we will repay you a thousand times."

The animals of Small Puddle wanted to help the poor animals of the Siberian pond. They said they would be pleased to do without the criminals, but the bear sent them anyway.

A year later, Big Frog called another meeting of the denizens of Small Puddle. Small Puddle had dried up considerably during the year, but there was still plenty of room. Of course the horses and the cows and sheep were absent, because they were engaged in international commerce. The mice and gophers and small birds had gone out for lunch with the eagle and had not yet returned. The trees around Small Puddle had all been logged, and the seeds and grains and berries had been collected and shipped to other ponds. Increasing trade had reduced the hog population, and the military practice from the armies of some of the great ponds had pretty much put an end to the flowers. On the brighter side, there were a lot more mosquitoes, and Big Frog was grateful for that. He was even fatter and sleeker than he had been before.

"Look around you," Big Frog told the tiny gathering of animals and birds that had not yet been part of international trade. "You will see that we are a meaner and leaner puddle. All the excess and flab of last year are gone. There are no animals loafing under trees and sniffing the flowers. We have the very latest in hardware and software and we are the possessors of items of miraculous engineering. We stand at the very edge of the wonderful future."

A couple of sheep who had not yet been slaughtered bleated a faint hurrah, but the fugitive mice and gophers who had hidden and refused to trade shouted out their boos.

Big Frog was outraged. "Some animals are without gratitude," he said to no one in particular. "They are completely without knowledge of their own self-interest."

He would have stayed to argue the point but he was already late. The hawk from the Gallic Pond had invited him out for lunch at a restaurant named La Grenouillère, where they specialized in frogs' legs, and where he was sure he would cut a fine figure.

THE PEACEABLE
KINGDOM

any years ago, in a time that was better than our own, there existed a peaceable kingdom on the shores of the northern sea. The animals of that kingdom went about their affairs without bothering each other, but they also cherished their differences. The rooster crowed the coming of dawn, and the sparrows celebrated the gathering dusk. A chorus of frogs announced the change of seasons, and cattle lowed peacefully in the afternoon. The beavers erected their dams and houses, and the flowers splashed a myriad of colours over the green of the fields. The grebes did a mating dance every spring that was so beautiful, the other animals were moved to tears by the sight.

And over it all, keeping everything together, was the Company of Black Crows. The crows announced the news every day, they brought the drama of life in the peaceable kingdom to all the inhabitants, and they continued to remind the animals that their kingdom was the finest kingdom in the world.

Then one year, not so very long ago, the wolf who had just recently been elected as leader of that country remarked to his friend the vulture, "Have you noticed that the Company of Black Crows seem to find fault with everything we do?"

"Friend Wolf," the vulture said, "You have hit the nail on the very head. The Black Crows are indeed our enemy. When we were in opposition, they paid little attention to our criticisms. Now that we are in power, they choose only to emphasize negative things, the number of members of our cabinet who have gone to prison, our friends who have received lucrative contracts, minor instances of corruption and malfeasance. It amounts to irresponsible conduct."

"They have become fat and complacent," the wolf said. "Perhaps they would have less time to criticize if they were hungrier."

"You may have noticed," said the vulture, "that they eat the very same food as vultures: garbage, carrion and road kill. And they get it all at public expense, eating it from roads that have been built and maintained by the state, while we in private life have to scour the countryside for the occasional corpse. It certainly isn't fair."

"Perhaps they would show more gratitude if we were to remove some of the carrion from the public roads," the wolf said. "It's worth an experiment."

And they did that. They withdrew some of the public support of the Company of Black Crows, and with fewer resources, the criticism grew less. The following year, they withdrew even more with the same salutary effect.

Some of the animals grumbled. They were accustomed to getting their news from the crows, and they didn't like the cutbacks. In the next election, the party of the wolf and the vulture was devastated. They received a mere two seats in the parliament of animals. Instead, the animals voted almost unanimously for the party of the sheep and the pig.

"Well, that was a successful election," the wolf said as he

wriggled out of his sheepskin. "I nearly suffocated in that costume. I wonder how sheep survive in all that wool."

"You're back," the pig exclaimed. "I thought surely you could never recover after the election."

"Well, I'm not the same wolf," the wolf told him. "But I am a wolf, and I do what wolves do. And I think that I'll begin by cutting back on the crows."

"Do you think that's wise?" the pig asked. "The crows are pretty hungry now. They might not survive another cutback."

"That's possible," the wolf answered. "Still, look at the bright side. The vultures will serve the role just as well. They have not so far been known for their public service, but I am sure if all the roadkill is available to them they will show their appreciation by providing the information the animals need. And they will be far less likely to criticize the government."

"I see that the vultures will be well served by this policy," the pig replied. "But what is in it for pigs? An ample supply of roadkill is neither here nor there when you are making a speech to a gathering of pigs."

"Songbirds," the wolf said.

"Songbirds?"

"Yes, indeed. What do songbirds eat?"

"Seeds," the pig replied. "Grain and corn, wheat and barley and oats."

"And what do pigs eat?"

"Grain and corn, wheat and barley and oats."

"Exactly," the wolf replied. "And there will be a side benefit. Have you ever been awakened by birdsong early in the morning after an evening in which you have consumed a quart or two of barley more than you should have?"

"All too often," the pig said. "Much to my regret."

"Well, if the supply of food to the songbirds is reduced, not only will there be more food for the pigs, there will be blissful silence in the mornings, and our evening walks will not be bothered by their noise."

It took little more than a nod in the direction of the deficit to convince the parliament of animals that they could not afford the luxury of birdsong, and the peaceable kingdom fell into silence.

The pig was satisfied, but a weasel who had been elected from one of the western provinces was not.

"Have you noticed the appalling increase in flagrant sexual display?" the weasel asked the wolf. "The religion of weasels demands that such things go on only when sanctioned by the One True Church of Weaseldom, and only in darkness and shame. And yet the grebes flaunt their disgusting passion in dances on the water. The grouse drums and puffs up his chest in the forest. The deer rut openly in the fields, and the orioles put on suits of orange for no reason other than sexual display. The peaceable kingdom is going mad with sexuality, and something must be done."

The wolf and the pig agreed. They spoke seriously to the parliament of animals of the terrible problem of the national debt, and they put a stop to dancing.

A surprising number of moles had also been elected, and they were anxious to see their own concerns addressed. They raised the problem of flowers. "This country is far too full of flowers," the spokesmole said. "Something has to be done. They use far too much soil that ought to be available to moles. Their roots get in the way of our digging. But worse than that, they have no purpose. They provide nothing but splashes of colour. Take, for instance, the huge bed of red flowers on parliament hill. What does it mean? What does it say to the animals of the peaceable kingdom?"

And, of course, nobody could quite say what it meant. Some of the animals argued that it was beautiful, and that beauty was a sufficient reason, but the wolf and the pig and the weasel and the moles all pointed out that beauty was fine for a rich country, but a country that was in debt could not afford anything as inessential as beauty. And, of course, the parliament of animals agreed.

Then a silence descended on the country. The crows no longer shouted out the news from one end of the land to the other. The vultures took on the crow's role, but they were much too busy eating to say anything. The birds kept their silence, and after a while, they forgot how to sing. Only a very few of the birds and animals continued to dance, and those who did, followed the example of the weasel and danced in the dark and in shame. The useless flowers were rooted from their beds, and the peaceable kingdom turned a uniform shade of brown.

For a while, the country went on in this way. The animals and birds felt that their self-denial was virtuous, and a better world would soon appear.

Then one day an eagle flew in from the south. The crows saw him, but they were too weak with hunger to tell anyone. The vultures thought he was only another vulture. But the eagle brought with him birds who could sing and animals who could dance, and he spread the land with the seeds of flowers. They were foreign birds and foreign animals and foreign flowers, but the animals of the peaceable kingdom had been starved for beauty for so long that they didn't care. They forgot that they themselves had once sung, that they had danced and they had cherished their own flowers. They forgot that there had ever been a peaceable kingdom, and they danced with the eagle. They danced. Danced. Danced.

Ukrainian Tales

AT BABI YAR

 obody has cut the grass at Babi Yar, and so there are wild flowers everywhere, white and yellow and blue. The deep depression in the ground surrounds the monument, but where there ought to be something angular as a correlative to all the pain suffered in this small acreage, there are only deep soft grass and wild flowers. Babi Yar is the centre point of cemeteries that stretch, it seems, for miles, military cemeteries, the graves crowded, the stones jostling each other in military fashion. These military graves have wreaths of cloth flowers, blue and yellow and white.

Bob and Dennis and I stand uneasy at the foot of the monument. Nobody can think of anything to say. Nothing can be said against the monstrous argument of Babi Yar, and so we seem to have mutually chosen silence.

Piotr walks uneasily around the monument. He wants one of us to ask him something, but none of us does. Finally, he says, "They told us that many Ukrainians had died here, that it was not only Jews, but we know now it was only Jews, or if they were Ukrainians they were also Jews." An old woman appears from the trees that line the left side of Babi Yar. She walks across the gravesite, up to the sidewalk, and continues down the road. There is no path, however. This does not seem to be a usual crossing. She has left footprints in the deep grass, but her crossing is no sacrilege. It is simply the fact that a woman who lives here has taken a shortcut, not one she usually takes, but perhaps she has reasons, this morning, to hurry.

The driver of the mini-van is smoking, and the smoke of his cigarette curls up, a blue wreath on the unusually still air. A couple of military vehicles, heavy shapeless trucks, rumble by, and he gets reluctantly out of their way.

I want to get this right. The sun is high, a clean morning light, and it is neither warm nor cold. There are buildings very near, houses, apartments and warehouses. We are only a few kilometres from central Kiev, still in the city, certainly. What happened at Babi Yar did not happen in some remote, unthinkable region where the trees are twisted and the wind can blow from anywhere. It happened in the heart of a thriving city.

How can anyone imagine a mass grave? The deep curved bowl of Babi Yar was once a mass of bodies, the dying and the dead, and now it is only a gap, an emptiness, a carpet of thick grass and wild flowers. I try to read the words on the monument, sound out the strange Cyrillic characters and find some meaning. Piotr translates the words into English for us, but even in our own language they refuse to signify, and I cannot remember a word now, the story as dead and gone as the Jews who died at Babi Yar.

We cannot stay forever. We have meetings to go to, and already we are late. I pick a small white flower, not from the flower bed but from the sloped shoulder of Babi Yar where it grows wild. I slip it into my lapel, making sure no one sees me. The gesture is so romantic and so inadequate, I do not want to explain it. Still I wear it all day, stubborn, I suppose. Neither Bob nor Dennis asks me anything about it, and I'm grateful for their tact. By evening it is faded and limp, and I should throw it away, yet I put it in my suitcase instead. By the time I get it back to

Canada it will be an unrecognizable lump of something or other, but I don't want to leave it behind.

Back in the mini-van, the driver makes a U-turn in the middle of the street. I am only now aware that the branches of the trees meet over the street, making it a dark tunnel. The cemetery on both sides of the road is dark too, the tall stones standing like soldiers at attention. Behind us, Babi Yar, for just that moment the brightest spot on the planet, slips into memory, and we turn right on the main street into traffic.

ONCE IN A SMALL BAR IN ODESSA

nce, in a small bar in Odessa, we drank beer that came in one-gallon pickling jars, and ate salted fishes whole. We sat on nail kegs at inverted wooden barrels in the noonday dark of the bar whose walls and ceilings were a single arc. Ukrainian and Polish sailors drank with swarthy Georgians and Azerbaijanis. Gambrinus. The bar where Kuprine drank his way through a Russian winter and dreamed the story of a small bar in Odessa.

Later, in Denmark, we caught a train to the ferry at Rødby. We chatted with a black Jamaican woman named Ingrid, who had just come from visiting her Norwegian grandmother. She recited a few phrases of Norwegian in a sing-song West Indian accent. The train was named Gambrinus. Jan Primus. The patron saint of beer.

We were tourists of course. Once you leave home you are always a tourist, however serious your business. They stared at us in the bar in Odessa, Lise, the only woman in the bar, dressed in a silver jumpsuit, her blonde hair tumbling over her shoulders like a waterfall. She might have been a space-age

Venus rising from the Black Sea. The sailors devoured her with their eyes.

"They will be robbed," Oleg said, gesturing in the direction of the Polish soldiers. "They are too eager for friends to drink with, too eager for someone who can speak Polish, someone who can help them to find love in Odessa."

The Black Sea rolls in with the power of any ocean. The waves crash so they seem heavier than water should be, black and more viscous. We waded in the cold water, the black water. Oleg stood disapproving at the limit of the waves. Lise went in too far, as she always does, raising her skirt nearly to her waist, but a wave caught her and she was drenched. The bored and nearly naked beauties of Odessa did not move where they lay on the sand, out of the bite of a crisp wind that had come from heaven knows where.

The driver of the mini-van would not let Lise enter his vehicle until I bribed him with a pack of Marlboros, the international medium of exchange. I don't smoke. Neither does he. Lord knows how many hands will hold this pack before somebody finally smokes it.

In the catacombs below the city, the hideouts of the heroic martyrs of the Second World War are waiting for tourists, but except for some local schoolchildren, we are the only ones there. Two Tanyas, one an expert on the catacombs, the other a speaker of English, lead us by the hidden machine guns to the rock beds where they slept, the deep dripped wax of their candles, these martyrs who did not see the light for two years, and then all they saw with the light they had dreamed of were the barrels of rifles.

In Kiev we had walked through the narrow catacombs holding before us the candles we had brought, down halls so narrow they brought me nearly to panic, past saint after shrunken saint blanketed in their tiny coffins. The catacombs of Odessa are higher, broader, wider, lit by electricity. If you straightened them out, they would run all the way to St. Petersburg. A wreath marks one black, unlit turning where a guide and a group of schoolchildren were lost.

"And never found?" we ask.

"Oh no!" the Tanyas tell us. "They were found. They must have been found. It could not have been otherwise."

At Gambrinus, the manager joins us for a beer. He is tall, thin and bald. He looks like a man who has failed at something higher and been reduced to this. A dancer, perhaps, or a poet. He was once a high government official, Oleg tells us. In some mysterious way he was disgraced, but since perestroika, he has hopes. The government seeks his advice, but he thinks in the brave new world that is coming, he will grow rich instead.

At the cottage in Denmark we learn about light. The yard is flooded with sunshine thick as marmalade. The trees and grass have tried out every shade of green, and the purple lilacs are seduced by the sunlight into releasing all their heavy fragrance into the air. In the forest beyond the garden, dappled light filters through the beeches, making the white blossoms of wild onions a crazy quilt. Small deer stare at us, wide-eyed and unafraid. At midnight we swim in the Baltic in absolute blackness, and the water is as cold as the Black Sea.

"Black as the grave in which my friend is laid," Lise says, and I think of Lowry drunk and brooding on the Pacific. Back at the cottage, we drink a bottle of Maltøl. It seems without alcohol, but Lise says it is an aphrodisiac.

Oleg tells us we must not stay too long at Gambrinus. The Black Sea sailors are famous for their violence, and it is true that they drink morosely and do not laugh. Kuprine must have sat at one of these tables, alone. I don't think the sailors would have joined him listening to the strains of a ghostly Jewish violin.

All this happens in late May, early June in the year of 199_. We leave Odessa for the small town of L____. Oleg introduces us to Stanislav, a poet who has walked from Washington to San Francisco without learning a word of English and with only his return ticket in his pocket. He did not spend a cent in America. His daughter Barbara, precocious and assured at nine years old, has several perfect English sentences. "How do you do? My name is Barbara. This is the town in which I live."

"I do not believe in the future," Stanislav tells us. "A Ukrainian who believes in the future is a fool. We are not meant to be free. We are meant to be brutalized and shot in the street like dogs."

"Stanislav believes in the future," Oleg says, after he has translated this. "He is a hopeless romantic."

"The coup has failed," Lise says. "The world is yours."

Stanislav wants to know what Lise has said. He has the trick of Ukrainian men of standing so close that he could kiss you in a moment if he wanted. Oleg translates, and Stanislav kisses Lise. He recites a poem at length. Oleg does not translate, but tells us that the poem is about a father's failure to return from the war. A son and a mother wait until all the returning soldiers have passed. When the father fails to arrive, the mother tells the son, "You are the father now."

"Yes," Barbara says. "He is my father."

It is my turn to recite a poem, but I know none of my own by heart. I can recite only British poems of Empire. "Horatio at the Bridge." "Tubal Cain." "Ozymandias." Stanislav wants me to recite Walt Whitman, but I can only tell him, that is another country.

Later that night at the Odessa Seaman's Club we drink Georgian cognac and play chess. I feel baroque and defensive. I play a King's Indian in the first game and we draw. As white, I play a Queen's Pawn Gambit, but Stanislav knows the game by Botvinnik, from which I have stolen it, and he beats me quickly. We are both drunk by the third game, and against his attack, I arrange my bishops in fianchetto. Full of contempt, he masses his forces in the centre and I pick off an errant knight. He cannot believe he has been so easily tricked. Oleg agrees. Stanislav would never allow such a thing to happen. Lise reminds them that he is playing with a capitalist and that he will have to spend the rest of his life looking over his shoulder for bishops.

And the next morning in the Hotel Krasnaya, the lobby was full of fat priests in black carrying wooden staves. Stanislav awakened us at seven, bringing sour buttermilk in triangular

Swedish paper cartons. He recites another poem, but Oleg is not there to translate it. This time I am ready and I respond with Alden Nowlan's "God Sour the Milk of the Knacking Wench." Stanislav is moved to tears. He kisses me full on the lips and leaves.

I tell Lise that this is an unusual experience for me. I have not kissed men before.

"Good," she says. "Did you like it?"

I have to think. "There was nothing unpleasant about it," I tell her. "Though I don't think I would initiate a repeat performance."

The fat priests seem to be waiting for someone of real importance. A black Volvo is parked on the sidewalk in front of the hotel. From somewhere in a hallway outside the lobby, a whining American voice rises over the subdued murmur of Russian and Ukrainian. "I was a sinner like you before I was saved," it says. "Then our Lord made me his own."

"He's insane," I tell Lise. "That is the voice of the certifiably mad."

"Yes, but you can't tell in North America," she answers. "The distinctions between sanity and madness are stretched so thin, you can never be sure. You have to come here to hear it."

Once, in the Fraserwood Hotel in Manitoba, the owner sat and drank with us on a dank October afternoon. The farmers in the bar all spoke to each other in Ukrainian. In the corner, an old man played a violin.

"We use six-row barley," the owner explained, "and we use a lot more corn. The barley makes it husky and the corn makes it sweet. That's the only difference between Canada and the States. Beer."

We drank toasts all afternoon, read our fortunes in the amber glasses, the sweet and husky beer. Jean the First invented the toast in the thirteenth century. Jean Primus. Gambrinus. The Flemish king of beer. The owner told us the story of a berry-picking expedition from Gimli to Grand Beach across Lake Winnipeg. Three pairs of lovers, the most beautiful and promising in the whole area in 1913, that last year of grace before the Great War. Their boat was swamped in a sudden summer storm, and they all drowned. They were found in couples clinging to each other in death. We toasted love.

In a small bar in Odessa we toast friendship. We eat salted fishes and drink the sweet and heavy Ukrainian beer that smells of new-mown hay. Oleg tells us that he will go to England soon as part of a group that is interested in peace. His way will be paid by the English, and they will give him forty pounds for his expenses. We toast England and peace.

The air in Gambrinus is heavy with the sweet scent of Russian tobacco. It drifts, a blue mist, above the heads of the drinking sailors. The ghost of Kuprine tilts his glass at me, and I tilt mine back. The sailors hum an eastern song, full of betrayal and loss, full of the sound of violins.

"Will you drown with me?" I ask Lise. "Wrap your arms around me and drift down through the dark currents of the Black Sea?"

"No," she answers. "Not in the Black Sea. Not in the Baltic. Not even in Lake Winnipeg. We've had enough of drowning." I can see the reflection of her face in my tumbler of beer, but whether the gold is in the liquid or her hair is impossible to say.

At the Grave of
Taras Shevchenko

hey were painting the ceiling of the lobby in the Hotel Krasnaya. A man sat at the top of a step-ladder about twenty feet high and by wobbling the legs of the ladder he was able to walk around and paint patches he couldn't otherwise reach. Lise said he looked like some kind of giant bird.

"It's ridiculously unsafe," Per told her. "If he falls off that, he's going to kill somebody." The lobby was filled with people who had to keep moving out of the painter's way as he wobbled his shaky ladder across the room. He seemed to be doing a sloppy job, and when Per handed in his key at the desk, he noticed that it was covered with drops of white paint. It was hard to tell whether the people in the lobby were also covered with paint. Per wiped his hand across his hair. Nothing. He must have escaped the universal paint-up.

Outside, the Chaika was waiting. It gleamed a malignant black among the grey and faded-blue Ladas and Skodas. Some party member's Volvo was the only competition, but it was a mere half the length of the Chaika, and the Chaika's driver gazed at the other driver with serene contempt. A pretty girl in a yellow dress with white polka dots rushed up to them.

"You are the delegation from Canada," she told them. "I am Natasha. I will be your guide today for the visit to the grave of Taras Shevchenko."

"We're not actually a delegation," Per told her. "We're just tourists."

"Yes," she said. "From Canada."

"Yes. And we thought maybe we wouldn't go anywhere today. Maybe we'll just walk around and do some shopping." The girl seemed confused, and her face darkened.

"My instructions are today at ten a.m. to take you to the grave of Taras Shevchenko."

"We'd sooner go shopping."

"You can't go shopping. It is necessary to have coupons to shop."

Per pulled a batch of coupons out of his pocket with a triumphant flourish. "You mean these?"

"How did you get those?"

"When I changed my money. The girl in the hotel gave them to me."

Natasha was even more confused now. Her face was flushed and she looked prettier than she had before. A little wisp of her dark hair curled into the corner of her mouth and she pushed it away with her tongue.

"This is very difficult," she said. Her accent was a delicate lilt, but it still resembled the fake accents of Boris and Natasha in the *Rocky and Bullwinkle Show*. "We have arranged to meet the deputy secretary of health for the Oblast. He is already waiting."

"Don't be difficult, Per," Lise said. "Let's go see Taras Shevchenko." She climbed into the back of the Chaika, and Per followed. Natasha stood outside and gave instructions to the driver.

"I think I'm falling in love," Per told Lise. "Did you notice those high cheekbones? Those black Slavic eyes?"

"Her eyes are blue," Lise said. "And she's not your type. Too imperious."

"I don't know. We could probably work it out. She could dress in leather and discipline me with small willow switches. We could buy a Doberman."

"Stick with open-faced blondes. I happen to know you don't like pain." Her blonde hair curled over her shoulders.

They drove through the streets of Kiev, past a demonstration at the central square where a couple of hundred men were waving their fists at a building across the street, past the golden domes of an ancient church and past the enormous figure of a worker that dominated the city. Natasha gave a running commentary that sounded as if it had been memorized in its entirety. She didn't even glance out the window as she described what they were passing.

Soon after they crossed the high bridge over the Dnieper, the Chaika pulled up at a bus stop and a short and very stocky man got into the car. He greeted them cheerfully and forcefully in Ukrainian. Natasha translated.

"He welcomes you to Ukraine. He hopes your journey has been happy and successful. His name is Vlodomir Domanski, but you may call him Vlodya. He is the deputy secretary of health for the Oblast, but he is also a poet. A lyric poet. He has published thirteen volumes of poetry. His subjects are love and nature. He would like you to tell him about your work."

"I write novels," Per said. "Detective novels and spy novels set in exotic locales."

"You do not," Lise said. "Don't believe him. He writes novels about young boys growing up on the farm, full of adolescent torment and sexual confusion. He's really good at sunsets and descriptions of geese flying south in the fall."

Natasha hesitated for a moment, then said something in Ukrainian.

"I have told him that you are a writer of prosaic," she said.

"That's right," Lise said. "That's him."

"When we get back to Canada," Per told Lise, "I am trading you in. I am going to send you back to Sweden and demand a replacement that is not defective in the areas of sympathy and simple human decency."

"You can't send me to Sweden," she answered. "My great-grandparents came over. My family has been Canadian longer than yours." She stuck her tongue out at him.

"The Swedes are famous for their warranties," Per said. "In a case as clear as this, I'm certain they'll stand behind the product."

They were out of the city now, past the airport and heading southeast. The road was lined with tall trees. The bottom of every tree was painted white. Per thought it looked like a scene near the beginning of Roman Polanski's film, *Knife in the Water*, except that it had been misty and raining in the film, and now there was brilliant sunshine. The fields along the road were lush and green. The crops, whatever crops they were, seemed to be flourishing. There were fewer cars now. Most of the traffic was motorcycles with sidecars. There was never anybody in any of the sidecars. They seemed to be filled with produce or boards or rusty machine parts, as if they were tiny pickup trucks.

The health secretary poet was talking to the driver, who was driving even faster now than he had driven during the week they had spent in Kiev. In the city, everything got out of the Chaika's way, but country drivers seemed more stubborn, and several times they had met other vehicles while passing, so they were three abreast on the narrow road.

"He was five times the driving champion of Ukraine," Natasha explained of the driver. "Now he is seventy-nine, but he still drives very fast." Natasha said this as if she were proud of him.

They pulled off the main road onto an even more narrow one that followed the Dnieper River. Here there were sand dunes and broad beaches. The river looked like a big blue lake, but there were no cottages and no pleasure boats. The fields were full of wild flowers, but there didn't seem to be any more crops. The vegetation had changed too. Now they passed evergreens and white trees that might have been poplars or birches.

They crossed the Dnieper again, and Per realized that they were passing over a hydroelectric dam. The broad stretch of water they had just followed was a lake created by the dam. They drove into a village at the far end of the dam, a large town actually, though the sign as they entered declared it a village. The streets of the village were crowded, and the people were all very well dressed. Many of them wore leather jackets and dresses. Pretty young women in miniskirts looked as if they were on their way to a party, though it was not yet noon.

"Why are Ukrainians so well dressed?" Lise asked Natasha. "I thought there were shortages. I thought you were supposed to be poor."

"There are shortages," Natasha answered. "We are poor. Yet everybody has fine clothes. That is our mystery."

"Yes, but how do you explain this mystery?"

"It cannot be explained. No one can explain it." The Chaika veered to the left and began to climb a steep gravel road so narrow that trees brushed against it. Vlodya began a long explanation of how difficult it was for a poet to have to be responsible for the health of twelve million people. Both of his subjects were denied him. He was too busy to fall in love, and he spent all his time in the city and did not get the opportunity to commune with nature. He hoped that this trip would allow him to write a poem.

"He must be planning on falling in love with you," Per whispered to Lise. "There won't be any nature at Taras Shevchenko's grave."

But there was nature. The grave itself was marked by an enormous statue of the poet, a monument about thirty feet high on a cliff overlooking the river. Red and yellow flowers outlined the borders, but they were almost swamped by the deep grass and wild flowers surrounding the area.

A small bald man arrived and shook their hands with considerable emotion. Natasha said that he had devoted his life to caring for Shevchenko's grave. He was always moved to meet great poets from other countries.

"Tell him I'm not a great poet," Per said. "Tell him I write detective novels."

Natasha conveyed the information, which brought tears to

the little man's eyes. He spoke at some length and came over and wrung Per's hand again.

"He is very moved," she said. "Mickey Spillane is his favourite author, and he hopes that your works will also be translated into Ukrainian so that he might read them. We have so little crime that there are no detectives, and so no one in the Soviet Union can write detective novels. But we have hope. Since perestroika we have many criminals, and soon we will have detectives to catch them. Detective novels will surely follow. We have no great criminals like you have in the United States, only moneychangers and extortionists right now."

"Tell him I'm not from the United States. Tell him I'm from Canada."

"He will not understand. We believe that Canada is a part of the United States."

"But it isn't."

"Nevertheless, that is what we believe."

"Maybe someday they'll put up a statue like this for you," Lise said. "Maybe half the streets in Canada will be named for you someday." Lise had wandered over to the wall at the edge of the cliff and she returned now to where Per was standing with Natasha and the detective-novel fan. Vlodya stuck so close to her that Per wondered whether he might not actually have fallen in love with her.

"No chance of that," Per told her. "If you admit you're a writer in Canada, they won't honour your credit cards. You have to pay cash in advance for everything."

"How about George Bowering?" Lise asked. "Maybe they'll put up a statue to George Bowering." She had heard Bowering read in Winnipeg once. As a rule, she didn't like writers, though she liked reading. Per never brought writers home for her to meet.

"Not even George Bowering. Not even Margaret Atwood. Maybe Margaret Laurence."

"Well, there's some hope then."

The party had drifted towards a big white building that turned out to be a museum. A very large elderly woman with steel-grey hair was introduced to them. She announced that she would be their guide to the museum. She was wearing a pin that said El Paso Texas. She explained that the city of El Paso had once had a Taras Shevchenko festival, and she had been invited to attend. Her English had a slight Texan accent.

She led them through the museum, reciting a description of the pictures and drawings on the wall as if she were a tape recorder. Per kept drifting away from the lecture to look at Shevchenko's drawings. They were really very good. Every time he moved away, however, the Texan voice lapsed into frosty silence until he returned. The secretary of health stayed so close to Lise that she appeared to be leading him on a leash.

They had a moment of freedom in a room full of tents and cooking equipment that looked as if it were meant to represent the Indians of western Canada, but was apparently a re-creation of the conditions in Tashkent or someplace where Shevchenko had been banished.

Lise joined Per behind the largest tent. "I think he asked me to sleep with him," she said. "He keeps whispering Russian into my ear."

"That's Ukrainian," Per told her.

"Whatever. It's certainly meant to be romantic."

In each room of the museum an old woman with gold teeth sat in a chair and watched that they didn't touch anything. The women all wore headscarves and heavy woollen sweaters, though it was very warm. The woman beside them now appeared deeply offended that they were talking, and she coughed loudly. The Texan was poised to begin speaking again, so they followed her into the next room.

Taras Shevchenko seemed to have had a lot of difficulties in life, but he also seemed to have had a lot of fun. The czar kept banishing him, but he kept coming back and having all kinds of love affairs. He was under sentence of death but seemed to be able to travel freely and was loved by everyone in the country.

"They're hopelessly inefficient," Per said. "In Canada or the States, if the government didn't like a poet and sentenced him to death, they wouldn't let him wander around like that. They'd catch him and put an end to it."

"But the people loved him," Natasha explained.

"Well, they don't love poets in the New World."

"Are you endangered?" Natasha asked.

"Not endangered. Simply ignored." Vlodya was standing beside a full-length portrait of Taras Shevchenko, and Per suddenly realized that he looked exactly like the poet. There was the same dark hair, the same stocky build. From a side view, they both had small but significant pot-bellies. Lise, standing beside him, was almost the same height. Her blonde hair and ivory skin were the exact opposite of his dark swarthiness.

On the way back they stopped at the cafeteria of a small zoo where the cook miraculously produced a banquet, though neither Per nor Lise could identify a single dish. Vlodya made elaborate toasts and tried to fill them up with vodka. As soon as any glass was not entirely full, he filled it up. When it was finally clear that neither Per nor Lise was going to get drunk in the middle of the afternoon, he went off with the driver to try to hunt down enough gasoline to get them back to Kiev. They sat on the banks of the Dnieper by the little zoo and watched the barges drift by.

"Did you notice that he looked exactly like Taras Shevchenko?" Per asked Lise.

"Yes. Do you think he's a reincarnation?"

"Probably. What are you going to do about his fascination with you?"

"I'll break his heart. That's what always happened to Taras."

"I thought Taras was successful with the ladies."

"You weren't paying attention. His heart was always being broken."

And that's what happened. When they got back to the hotel at the corner of Taras Shevchenko and Pushkin streets, Natasha took Lise aside and delivered Vlodya's declaration of love. Per went up to their room alone so that no one would be embarrassed. Lise declined the kind offer, but thanked

Vlodya for the compliment, and he went away to try to mend his broken heart.

There was no hot water in the room, and Per was cursing from the bathroom, where he had just discovered this fact. "What can you say about a country that can't provide hot water in a luxury hotel?" he said.

"You can say that they love poets, that poets can be elected as leaders and that it is still possible to be a mad romantic," Lise answered.

"Right," Per answered, walking into the room, his naked body dripping cold water. "Next week, Odessa, and if it's as good as this we'll move here for keeps."

Fabulations

Tansy From My Garden

ut tansy in my coffin," she said. "When I die, put tansy in my coffin, and bury me with my head to the north so I can face the sun."

"Why tansy?" I asked her. "Why not rosemary? Why not rue?"

"Tansy for immortality," she said. "Tansy for sprained ankles, tansy for varicose veins, tansy to remove freckles. Once I was freckled. Did you know that? A poultice of tansy and all the freckles went away."

"Why not rue?" I insisted. "Why not the herb of grace that I stole from my neighbour's garden?"

"Too dangerous for pregnant women," she answered. "But it keeps away fleas and flies."

"But so is tansy," I told her. "Tansy is also dangerous for pregnant women. Though you are not pregnanat. What do you say about that?"

"Rue for snakebite," she said. "Rue to keep away the plague, though to tell you the truth, I don't much fear the plague, what with penicillin and all."

I went out to the garden. The tansy was spreading its green

ferns, but it was only mid-June and the yellow flowers had not yet appeared. The rue was healthy, but still small. Its yellow flowers hadn't appeared either. The rue was next to the rosemary, but sage and savory and sorrel separated it from the tansy. I had planted the herbs alphabetically this year, in case I forgot one of the names. Then I could just check the index of my book on herbs, and I could figure out the name of whatever I had missed. Last year I planted by the colour of flowers, and the rue and the tansy were in the yellow garden, along with the chamomile, the calendula and the sweet bay. I even tried growing dandelions and wormwood for the colours of the flowers, but they weren't successful.

In the field behind the house, a bobolink trills his unfaithful melody. He's keeping a harem, a half dozen nests with wives tending to his indiscriminate progeny. No wonder his warble is so sweet. The bobolink is white above and black below, as if someone had explained camouflage to him, and he'd got it backwards. He was thinking of all that wooing he had to do, and so he wasn't paying attention.

"You still have freckles," I told her when I came in from the garden. "You've always had freckles. A saddle of freckles across your nose."

"I'll need another poultice," she said. "Fresh tansy from the garden. I'll take care of it next Thursday."

"Next Thursday you are going to Düsseldorf," I reminded her. "And just when the basil will be ready."

"Wednesday, then. Wednesday, I'll take care of the freckles."

"And I will have to make the pesto myself," I told her, unable to hide a note of bitterness in my voice. "I will have to pick the tender leaves and grind the garlic and shred the cheese and pour the olive oil. And we have no pine nuts. Did you know that we were completely out of pine nuts?"

"I have wide eyes," she said. "My face is five eyes' width. And my eyes are hazel. Both are said to be signs of beauty."

"Yes," I agreed. "You are beautiful, freckles and all, though your eyes are blue. Tell me again why you are going to Düsseldorf."

"Windows," she said. "It has to do with windows. Sandblasted and sculptured glass. Glass that has been stained with colours. Glass so clear you cannot know it is there. Glass that is impervious to bugs and spiders and the unfortunate droppings of birds. And doors. Doors with glass in them. Windows and doors. And walnuts will work just as well as pine nuts. We have all the walnuts your heart could desire."

"It's not a question of expediency," I told her. "I know we have walnuts. We also have hazelnuts and almonds. It's a matter of principle. If you do not have pine nuts, can you really claim to have pesto?"

"Walnuts have an even richer history as regards pesto than pine nuts," she said. "Tradition counts for something."

In the shower Thursday morning, I sang in my rich baritone, "See the pyramids along the Nile." You remember the song. It has a bittersweet, rueful tang to it, and since I am not an early riser, I often find myself a touch melancholy in the shower.

"Was that meant for me?" she asked, when I came out of the shower, smelling masculine and pure from the strong soap I habitually use. "Are you sending me subliminal musical messages from the bathroom while I am preparing for a gruelling business trip in Europe?"

"Nothing of the sort," I told her. "In the shower, my heart is entirely pure. Later in the day, you might have to deal with some mild duplicity, but in the morning I am incapable of subtlety."

Her freckles had disappeared. Her face was entirely clear.

"I prefer the freckles," I told her. "They make you look wholesome and healthy. The daughter of a farmer. Someone close to nature."

"Good," she said. "Plant another row of tansy."

"That business about tansy in your coffin," I asked. "Was that modish *fin de siècle* morbidity, or are you worried about flying across the Atlantic?"

"You always miss the point," she said. And I drove her to the airport and waited in the parking lot until her plane left the ground without incident and turned its nose towards Europe. Nasturtium is the nose twister.

"Remember me," I crooned in the shower, "when the nights

are cold and lonely." The water pressure was low and that meant I'd have to go down into the basement and adjust the pump again. "Remember me, when you're by the riverside." I think I may have made up the second line myself. I've never heard anyone else sing it.

Rosemary for remembrance. By now she would have arrived in Düsseldorf. She would have unpacked her bags and discovered the sachet of rosemary I sent along. "Oh, Rosemarie, I love you," I sang. Sea mist. The old queen of Hungary made so beautiful by rosemary that she was still receiving proposals on her deathbed.

The radio announced that a jet had crashed on landing at the Düsseldorf airport. A minor crash, only seven dead. No mention of Canadians among them. The telephone rang. I bruised my shin on the way to answer it. They were concerned about my rugs. They wanted to wash them with a new patented method that would remove the deep-down dirt.

"No," I said. "Thank you. I have other things on my mind."

"Your plantain leaf is excellent for that," Romeo told Benvolio, "for your broken shin." I limped all morning as I telephoned numbers for information.

"There is no information," they told me. "It was a domestic Lufthansa flight from Frankfurt to Düsseldorf. There is no report of Canadians aboard."

"If it was a domestic flight," I said, "they might not know whether or not there were Canadians aboard."

"Yes," they agreed. It was possible the authorities might not know.

Bitter gall and wormwood. The idea of the lover's death is more horrible than the idea of your own passing. Wormwood grows everywhere. On moonlit nights it shimmers silver in the fields. We call it wild sage in these parts. I could brew myself absinthe, and die like a French artist, earless perhaps, or simply rotting in Marseille. The monks put wormwood in their ink to poison it so that mice would not eat their precious words. Even language has its dangers.

I would have to intervene with the gods, I knew that. There

was no point in trusting to earthbound authorities. If a phone call came and announced that she was dead, then she would be dead, and nothing could recover her. The earthbound authorities live in a world where there is only one possibility at any given time. The gods are more flexible.

Ganymede, the cupbearer to Zeus, was transformed by a potion from a mortal to a god. The key ingredient was tansy. I gathered tansy from my garden, lavender for the flavour, lovage for emotion, sweet bay for protection, and anise as good measure to protect me from my own brew. Tansy, I am told, contains thujone, a relative of the THC that makes marijuana so delightful, but a misplaced molecule or two converts it into a deadly poison. Still, if you are going to talk with the gods, you have to take some chances.

I brewed my tea, adding just a scant teaspoon of sugar to take off the edge, and if I must confess, yes, I also added scotch, a single malt I had been saving for some unimaginably important event. I drank and slept, and I suppose I must have intervened with the gods while I slept, because the telephone awakened me.

It's always one thing or the other. The news is good or bad. You have won or lost. It was she on the telephone, safe in Düsseldorf, exhausted by the flight and by a day of meetings, but somehow strangely exhilarated. She felt, she said, reborn.

I asked her about the crash, and she said I had it all wrong. The plane had crashed at Dortmund, not at Düsseldorf. Seven were injured, but no one had died. The glass-makers of Düsseldorf, those masters of windows and doors, were as good as they had promised. Their glass was clean and clear.

"Have the freckles returned?" I asked her.

She said they had.

"I have plucked all the tansy from my garden," I told her. "Not a leaf remains. You will have to put up with freckles for another season." I did not tell her of my intervention with the gods. Some things are best left unsaid.

"I think I may be pregnant," she said. "I have no symptoms, but I am irrationally convinced that I am."

"Good," I answered. "Then I'll pluck out all the rue as well."

BAD GIRL

nce upon a time in a small town just near the Saskatchewan border, there lived a very disobedient girl. Her name was Ellen, and she was in grade twelve. She wanted to go to university to study music and become a famous singer, but her mother wanted her to get a job in town as a clerk in the Co-op store, and her father wanted her to stay on the farm and help her mother with the milking and the chickens. They were both deeply religious people, and they were afraid that if Ellen went out into the wide world, she would lose her religion and come to harm.

"I don't know how many times I've told you," her mother would say, "but I'm telling you again. If you wear your skirts as short as you do, you are asking for trouble."

"Don't talk back to me, young woman," her father said almost every day. "And don't flash your eyes at me. I know insolence when I see it, and I won't tolerate it, do you understand?"

Ellen knew she was disobedient. She was supposed to pray in a soft voice at the beginning of each class, but she hadn't done so for years, and nothing had happened to her. She had sneaked off and gone to a movie with the other kids, and God had not struck her dead. She'd even had a glass of rye whisky with some of the boys at a dance to which she had been forbidden to go, and she had not got drunk and the police had not caught her.

In fact, it seemed that the only bad things that ever happened to her were delivered by her own parents. Ellen's mother liked to slap her when she didn't work hard enough. Her father beat her whenever he found out that she'd done something he didn't like. But everybody else in town was good to her, and they all loved to hear her sing. They said things like, "You've got the voice of an angel. You should study and become an opera singer."

Her parents warned her that God watched her every move, and that he would not be mocked. He would deliver pain for disobedience.

"If that's the case," Ellen said to herself, "then my parents must be working off a lifetime of disobedience."

And that seemed as if it might be true. Her father went to church every Sunday, but the bank was threatening to take away the farm, and he'd broken his leg when he rolled the tractor, and now he walked with a painful limp. Her mother had varicose veins and some sort of stomach disease that made her breath smell so bad that nobody wanted to sit next to her, not even in church. If they were God's chosen, Ellen decided, then she'd just as soon escape his notice.

Ellen got straight A's in grade twelve. School work came easy to her, and she liked the classroom, where everyone was polite to each other, and where you really did seem to get what you deserved. If you worked hard, you got an A. If you didn't, you got a B or a C. if you didn't do anything at all, you failed.

Ellen's biggest disobedience was the secret bank account she kept. She was working part-time at the Co-op and saving up to go to university. If she won a couple of scholarships, she was sure that she could do it. Her greatest fear was that her parents might find out about her bank account and seize it. It would be a month until she turned eighteen, and she wasn't sure whether her parents could steal her money or not. The one thing she was certain about was that if they found out, religious or not, they would take her money from her.

The other problem was Larry. Larry was madly in love with Ellen and he wanted to marry her. Ellen knew that her parents would forbid the marriage at first, but she was pretty certain that they'd finally give in. It was the one place that she was hoping for their rigidity. If she married Larry, then she would never be a famous singer. She would be a farm wife just like her mother, and she would become dry and mean and get varicose veins and bad breath.

About a month earlier, Larry had become so insistent about marrying her that the only way she could convince him not to go to her father and ask for her hand was to sleep with him. Or not so much sleep with as have sex with in the back seat of his Chevy. Ellen had been worried that she would get pregnant, and her mother had warned her so often about sex that she assumed it would be a painful and horrible experience.

It turned out to be the most fun she'd ever had. She couldn't believe how nice it was, and after the first time, she walked around like Marco Polo must have when he discovered China. She could hardly think about anything else, and for a couple of weeks, she didn't do anything to anger either of her parents. She almost agreed to marry Larry.

Her father noticed her change of mood and became very watchful. He drove his pickup into town and spied on Ellen when she went for lunch to the Chinese café, and he insisted that she come right home from school and not go out in the evening. Ellen didn't care. She had sex with Larry standing up in the janitor's room during study period.

Ellen's father talked to Ellen's mother, and Ellen's mother took her aside and talked to her about sex. Ellen could barely stand the smell of her mother's breath, but she listened.

"I just want you to be careful," her mother said. "If you lose your reputation, then nobody will want to marry you. Your father and I would just die if you got pregnant. We couldn't hold up our heads in church. And don't think it's any great deal. It's something a woman has to suffer, and there's no point to starting suffering any sooner than you need. And you are the church organist. Remember that."

Ellen did not forget that she was the church organist. It was the single good thing that she could say about the church. Her father would never have let her continue to take lessons if it weren't that it made him look good at church. Sometimes, when she was playing a hymn and she saw her father standing in the first pew, singing off-key in his whiny voice, she imagined him keeling over with a heart attack. She wouldn't even stop playing. She'd switch into something joyful and triumphant with great crescendos.

Ellen felt that the best way to avoid suspicion was to be as disobedient as her parents wanted. So she didn't do the dishes she was supposed to do, and she didn't feed the calves, and her mother slapped her. She took the car without permission on a Sunday afternoon and made love to Larry in a haystack, and got back late for supper. Her father beat her with his belt, and made her pray on her knees for two hours, but he stopped following her around and spying on her with his binoculars.

When the school year came to an end, the principal told her father that she'd won a thousand-dollar scholarship.

"Good," her father said. "She can buy herself a couple of calves and raise them over winter." The principal told him that she could only use the money to go to the university.

"How about Bible college?" her father asked.

"Well, yes, I suppose," the principal answered. "But I thought she wanted to study music."

"Got her heart set on Bible college," her father said, and he went home and announced to Ellen that she would be attending Thorncrest Pentecostal Bible College.

"Got your heart set on an education. Well, this is the only education that really counts," he told her. "It'll teach you a little about authority and discipline."

Ellen felt that she would sooner go to prison than to Bible college. She would sooner work in the Co-op or help around the farm. But it gave her an excuse to apply to the university. You had to be accepted at the university to get into Thorncrest, she would tell her parents if they asked. She had applied for several bursaries and a government loan, and when the letters of reply came from the university, she managed to sneak the answers by her father by getting to the mailbox first and hiding the responses in her room.

In the meanwhile, Larry was nearly frantic about her going away to the city to study at Bible college. He wanted her to stay home and marry him, and when she told him that she wasn't ready to make that sort of commitment and maybe they could just be friends, he wept and then raged, and told her that she'd be married to him by fall, just you wait and see.

Things came to a crisis the day before her birthday. Larry caught her on the way back from the Co-op, and announced that he couldn't live without her, and that if she didn't agree to marry him, he was going to kill her and commit suicide. He showed her the shotgun he had bought for the occasion. Ellen agreed to marry him of course, but she convinced him not to tell her parents until the morning of her birthday. He agreed to wait a day, but no longer.

When she got home, her father was waiting for her. He waved a sheaf of papers at her. "I've been in your room," he said. "Checking for drugs because you've been acting so strange. And I found these."

"Those are my applications for Thorncrest College."

"It doesn't say Thorncrest College. It says university."

Ellen wasn't sure how much her father knew about the application process, but her only hope was to bluff. "It has to say university. First you get accepted to the university. Then when you get there, you fill out a form for Thorncrest College."

"Well it don't explain this," he said, waving her bankbook in the air. "It don't explain how you got four thousand dollars in the bank."

"I earned it, working at the Co-op and babysitting. It's my money." Ellen's heart sank as she saw her hopes for escape dimming. Even Larry suddenly loomed as hope.

"Stole it you mean," her father said. "You've been eating my food and living in my house with all that money in the bank and me nearly crazy trying to find a way to feed you. You owe me that for room and board."

"Your father's right," her mother chimed in. "That's properly our money."

"And we're going straight down to the bank to get it," her father added, and he caught Ellen by the wrist and dragged her out to the pickup. When they got to town, he hauled her from the truck and dragged her to the door.

"Now you get that money and bring it directly out," her father said.

Ellen reached out her hand and pulled the door handle. It wouldn't open. The tellers in the bank were all at their stations, counting their change, but she could see that the clock on the wall read one minute after three.

"It's locked," she said. "It closes at three on Mondays. We'll have to wait until tomorrow."

"We're getting it now," her father shouted, and he began to hammer on the door of the bank. At first there was no answer. Finally, the manager came to the door and spoke to them through an electronic box.

"We're closed," he said in a tinny electronic voice.

"Well, open. We got some banking to do."

"I'm sorry. You'll have to wait until tomorrow."

"Open that door. We're coming in now." Ellen's father was livid with rage. The manager, on the other side of the glass door, seemed equally livid.

"I'm calling the police," he said. "The teller has already called them. You can't force a bank to open when it's closed."

"Call them, then," Ellen's father shouted at the door. "They can take away this thieving slut until I get my money back from her." And he turned to glare at the spot where Ellen had been standing only a moment before. There was nobody there, and the pickup was gone.

Ellen drove home as fast as she could, skidding on the gravel of the driveway as she rounded the corner. Her mother was out in the barn, or perhaps in the chicken house. At least she wasn't in the house, and Ellen was grateful for that. She tossed clothes at random into a suitcase, and collected all her papers with their acceptances and bursaries and put them in too. Then she put on her shortest skirt and walked to the highway and stuck out her thumb. The first car that came along picked her up and gave her a ride all the way to the city. She stopped at the first bank she came to and used her bank card to withdraw three hundred dollars. Then she spent her first night away from home in a Holiday Inn. She swam in the pool, and she ordered breakfast in bed for the next morning. She felt no guilt. She felt only a sense of peace that she had always known was waiting for her somewhere.

Her father disowned her, as she had hoped he would. He put a message in the local paper saying that he was no longer responsible for her debts, and she read it in the university library. But he didn't pursue her any farther, and no police came to her door. Larry disappeared into the past as if he had been erased from a sheet of paper. After the second day, she could hardly remember his face. Ellen moved in with a medical student who thought he was poor, but he paid the rent and he was a decent lover.

Ellen did not see Larry or either of her parents after that final day, and she didn't think she ever would. There was, however, one brief electronic moment when they were together. Ellen's parents had gone to the Legion to play bingo. Larry was the caller. At intermission, he turned on the big television at the front of the hall. Ellen appeared on the screen in the role of Carmen. She was dressed in a revealing cotton dress and was sitting on a low stool. Her rich voice filled the hall for just one second before Larry turned the switch and put on the hockey game.

Ellen perched carefully on the side of the bed so as not to awaken her lover. From the window of the villa, she could see the sun glint on the Mediterranean waves. Ellen's parents straightened their cards. Larry's voice began, "Under the B, six."

QUOTIDIAN

 t didn't seem like such a big deal, leaving his wife and moving in with Susan. Jim was forty and restless. It was time to put some order into his life. Julia, his wife, was a big woman, not fat but what people called raw-boned. She'd grown up on a farm and ridden horses, and she didn't like a lot of nonsense. People thought she was a hippie when she was young, because she didn't like bras or shaving her armpits or wearing make-up, but that wasn't it. She'd have done the same thing even if the hippies hadn't come along.

Susan, on the other hand, smelled like his mother's friends, as he remembered them from his childhood. He remembered mostly his head being pulled into a bosom smelling of powder and perfume and rough with lace. "Goodbye," his mother's friends said, "goodbye, goodbye," and they pulled his face between their breasts and kissed him on the top of the head. Their perfume was cheap, mostly Evening in Paris, about the only kind you could buy in a small town in those days. It came in a bright blue bottle, and he'd always bought it for his mother at Christmas.

Susan wore Alfred Sung, and she dressed in narrow suits with expensive blouses, but it was really the same thing on a higher level. The first time he met her, he wanted nothing more than to sink his head between her breasts, feel the lace on his cheeks and smell the perfume. She was surprised by him, amazed that he wanted her so much. She said that she'd had lots of boyfriends but nobody had ever fallen quite that much in love with her. And she left her husband for him, just like that.

And yet it wasn't really love or even desire, though there was some of that. He hardly knew her. They'd met at a party at the Baileys' at Christmas, and here it was March and the snow hadn't even gone and they were living together. They'd had coffee together three times between Christmas and New Year's, and made love for the first time in a motel on the morning of January the third. She'd never done anything like that before, she said. And she'd gone out and bought all new underwear for the occasion, and he loved her for that.

Julia said she was going to take him for everything he had, but he didn't mind. He was glad to get out from under the weight of all those possessions. He took his clothes, but she wouldn't give him anything else, not even the camera she'd given him for Christmas, or his old umbrella. His lawyer said that this was nonsense, he could get half of everything, but he said no, let her have it. Contest nothing. Not even the books, which he needed. He could buy new books to teach his classes from. And they wouldn't have his old notes scribbled in the margins.

So when they moved into the apartment, they had very little furniture, just the things that Susan had brought: a bed, a chest of drawers, a chesterfield and chair, a dining-room table and four chairs, a coffee table and a few lamps. He was delighted by the built-in bookcase with no books in it, just an Eskimo sculpture and a couple of ceramic birds. Every night, he threw out the newspapers so they wouldn't accumulate.

One morning, Susan served him *café au lait*. She made espresso in a little Italian coffee maker and heated up milk in the microwave. She mixed them together, added a full tea-spoon of sugar, and served the coffee in big blue flowered bowls. Jim loved it. It reminded him of his childhood as much as the perfume did. He remembered sitting at a bench behind his grandmother's table and being served sweet milky coffee while the grown-ups chatted about the kind of things they talked about in those days. He fell in love even more deeply than he had been before, though that didn't seem possible.

"Just like Paris," Susan said. "Wouldn't it be great to be sitting at a little outdoor café in Paris, just the two of us, drinking *café au lait* and eating a baguette with strawberry jam?" She tilted her face forward so that her carved chin caught the morning light, like a model in *Elle* magazine. Jim recognized the scenario all right. He'd seen it in a million magazines, but he had never imagined himself in the scene.

"Paris," he agreed. "*Café au lait* and baguettes in the morning, and the Folies Bergères in the evening. But what do you do in Paris in the middle of the day after you've visited la Tour Eiffel?"

"You shop," Susan said. "You walk up and down the Champs-Elysées and look at all the beautiful clothing, and you stop in at the perfume shops and spray yourself with perfume so expensive you could never afford to buy it."

"I'll buy you some," Jim told her. "I'll fly to Paris and bring you back the most expensive perfume they've got."

"Don't be silly. We've barely got the money to pay the rent. I'll settle for a subscription to *Vogue*. That's about as close as I'll ever get to high fashion in this lifetime."

Susan was right. They were short of money, though Jim hoped that the situation would be temporary. He had his job, teaching communications at the community college. Julia wouldn't give him any of the things they owned, but she hadn't asked for any money. And anyway, she earned as much as he did, so the judge probably wouldn't have given her a lot even if she'd wanted it. Jim was paying off the loan on the Honda, but that would be over in a couple of months.

He realized that he and Susan had never really discussed finances. They were sharing the costs of the apartment and the food because Susan had insisted she did not want to give up her independence. It struck him that he had not bought any-thing for the apartment. But that was not because he couldn't afford it. He just didn't want anything more in the place. He had nearly fifteen thousand dollars in a savings account he had never even told Julia about. But, of course, Susan didn't know about it either.

And come to think of it, he didn't know where Susan's money came from. She hadn't worked for several years. He thought she'd said she was once a legal secretary, but he wasn't sure. Maybe Bert was paying her. Bert was her husband, or soon to be ex-husband. He taught in the same department as Jim at the college, and even though he'd been really upset when Susan first left him and had threatened to kill Jim, he didn't seem to hold any hard feelings once the matter was settled and Susan had actually moved out. He'd bought himself a little Mazda convertible and was seriously courting the head of the Business Science department, a woman who owned a number of low-rental apartments and spent her holidays at a place she owned in Costa Rica. Bert liked to tell Jim about their lovemaking with a nudge, saying, "Now there's a real woman." Behind it, of course, was the implication that they both knew Susan was not that. Jim was tempted to tell Bert that if he regarded lovemaking as primarily an athletic event, he could recommend Julia, but he never did.

He did brood about Susan and Paris, however. He didn't like to think that she was living her life second-hand, that there was something for which she yearned that she had already accepted as impossible. And because he had the money in the bank to make her dream possible, it seemed to him mean-spirited not to use it.

Still, he felt some reluctance. He had started the fund for an emergency, a backup for some unimaginable disaster, and he was reluctant to lose the security. Jim wasn't stingy. He thought of himself as generous, and yet he had a sense that, somehow, he paid for more than his share of everything.

And yet, what kind of disaster was possible? He had no children, his parents were in good financial shape, his job was secure. The money might be better used as a gesture of generosity than as a hedge against the future. In fact, the more he thought about it, the making of a grand gesture was a more noble thing than some accountant-like squirrelling away of cash.

Against this was a growing realization that a trip to Paris might be more than a gift to Susan. Paris was the centre of the things that moved him most deeply: perfume, sweet coffee, the spare and elegant arrangement of things. Maybe he could find out something about his dreams if he went directly to their source.

But first, it was important to find out where Susan's money came from. It came from her father, she said, from some sort of investment he had set up for her out of a small inheritance she had received from her grandmother. The interest came to a couple of thousand dollars a month.

Jim calculated. That meant a lot of money invested, but she told him no. Enough to buy a small car, she thought. She couldn't remember the figures, but it was not much. It was just that her father was good at investing. Jim was pretty sure nobody was that good at investing, but he didn't press the issue.

Things were going better at work. Jim had all new books without notes in them, and it seemed that his lectures had improved now that he had to make new ones from scratch. His students were more enthusiastic than they had been in years. Susan had started looking for a job, though she was pretty vague about what she had decided to do.

One day she came home and told him she had got a job as a shopper. She worked for a company that bought things for women executives who were too busy to do their own shopping. Everything from groceries to undergarments. Jim had trouble believing such a job existed, but Susan went off to work every morning, and she had a business card that said La Chance Import. And she had a credit card to buy all the things she was asked to shop for. Jim grew increasingly restless. He wanted Susan to have all those beautiful things, but he knew he could not pay for them.

Sometimes she would bring things home for the evening: business suits, party dresses, coloured scarves, flashy earrings, gold necklaces, watches and rings, lingerie that even Jim could tell was expensive. She never tried anything on, though. That would violate the contract, she said. The clothes would then be second-hand.

And so, of course, they went to Paris. Susan objected that it was impossible, that they didn't have enough money, but once Jim had brought the tickets home and convinced her to have her picture taken and to send off for her passport, she seemed to lose any curiosity about the source of the money.

There were two Parises. Actually, there are a great deal many more than two, but two were all Jim and Susan discovered. One was the Paris of the left bank, where lovers loved in broad daylight and students studied in the little cafés near the Sorbonne. Here, tourists merged with exiles from abroad and exiles from other parts of France, and the very air proclaimed that anything was possible, that nothing was permanent. The ghosts of Hemingway and Joyce skittered around corners, just out of sight, and a thousand Lady Bretts, their bullfighters in tow, got drunk in dark bistros.

The other was the Paris of the rich, the Champs-Elysées, the impossibly expensive hotels where only Arab princes and Canadian prime ministers could afford to spend a night. Strange, beautiful people got out of dark limousines so expensive that they did not advertise their names. Somebody met them at doorways and ushered them into rooms where there was no admittance to the public. Jewellery in windows and the clothing in stores made the entire cost of Jim and Susan's trip seem trivial. Somewhere, a life of beauty and privilege was being lived, and here was a node where travellers from Parnassus touched briefly down on earth.

Jim wanted them to spend as much time as possible along the golden avenues. He wanted Susan to be happy, and he thought she might learn things about style that would help her in her job as a shopper. Susan wanted to spend most of the time along the rue Monge and the rue Saint-Jacques and the boulevard Saint-Germain.

"You'll be able to tell your students that you were in the same bar where Hemingway and Fitzgerald argued," she said. "You'll be able to tell them what it's really like."

But when they got home to Winnipeg, Jim could think only of the glimpse of great wealth he had seen, and Susan was obsessed by *la vie bohémiènne*. She quit her job as a shopper and enrolled at the art school. She started to take acting classes. She filled the bookshelves with books about art. She made a new set of friends who had long hair and who pierced sensitive parts of their bodies and decorated themselves with cheap jewellery. The apartment was strewn with half-finished canvases and jars of paint and turpentine. She found little cafés where people read poetry and played saxophones, and she was happy.

Jim panicked. The simple order he yearned for had disappeared. He no longer recognized the woman he was living with, and she in turn seemed to regard him with something not far from contempt. His students didn't care about Paris. All the places they wanted to go were destinations in cyberspace, and Jim couldn't even operate a computer. He began to think about death, and before long he could think of almost nothing else. It seemed to him that he had been born into the wrong world and that he would die before getting any more than a glimpse of the only one that really mattered.

And then he won the lottery. Fourteen million dollars. Things like that do sometimes happen. They happen to ordinary people. Why not Jim?

He offered to divide the money with Susan, but she only laughed. She wasn't interested in money. She left him and moved in with a sculptor who also played the cello, and she became immediately pregnant. Jim quit his job at the college, and set out to be rich.

Nothing happened. A few charities sent him letters asking for money, but nobody seemed particularly interested in being his friend. The beautiful people did not cluster around him.

When he went to stores, even though he had a great deal of money, he had to use the same entrance as everyone else. He tried to buy a very expensive car, but he was put on a waiting list and told it would be at least two years before it could be delivered.

Winnipeg, it seemed, was not a good place to be rich, though when he looked around, he did see rich and beautiful people. They, however, did not seem to see him.

He moved to Paris. He rented the same suite that the prime minister of Canada had made momentarily famous by sleeping in it while children starved. He rented an expensive car and drove down the Champs-Elysées, but only a few passing tourists cared. He went to Switzerland to ski, and he saw British royalty and famous actresses, but none of them saw him. He couldn't get reservations at famous restaurants no matter how much he was prepared to tip.

His money began to oppress him. Every time he bought something, he had another object that needed to be kept somewhere. The objects cried out for him to use them, but he didn't want to. He wanted to take a princess through the private entrance to a store in Paris and buy her jewellery, but he couldn't meet any princesses, and he couldn't find the private entrances.

Finally, he returned to Winnipeg. He bought himself a penthouse in the most expensive block he could find, and he painted it white inside, and put in white rugs and a white grand piano just like the one he had seen in a picture of John Lennon's apartment. Then he sat and waited.

And one day there was a knock on the door. The woman who confronted Jim when he opened the door was a little overweight, and her accent was very strong and completely unidentifiable. She was collecting for the United Way, and she loved Jim's apartment. Her name, she said, was Leila Schranz-Lohmeyer.

Jim gave the United Way five thousand dollars, and he took Leila out for dinner. She was, she said, a princess of the deposed Bulgarian royal family. She chose the most expensive food on the menu, but she only picked at it. They talked about Paris, and she yearned for the days of her girlhood, playing along the Champs-Elysées while her mother shopped.

Jim decided to gamble. He told her almost nothing of his trips to Paris, but he took her there and asked her to make arrangements to shop while he dealt with some business. Later that afternoon they were picked up in a limousine and driven to a store, where they were ushered through the private entrance to a floor where the clothes were even more expensive than those he had seen before. That evening they dined with a count and a famous musician whose name Jim thought he had read somewhere in a magazine. Of course, he paid for everything.

They went skiing in Switzerland, and dined with a famous Hungarian actress and tennis player from Poland who had been a sensation a few years ago. Everybody had a double-barrelled name and a strong accent, though Jim could never quite identify the accents. Nobody ever spoke of money, or offered to pay for anything.

When they got back to Winnipeg, Leila stripped the penthouse even more bare than it had been. She threw out most of the few mementoes Jim had saved from his childhood and his previous two marriages. Her own bedroom, the room she called her boudoir, was wildly chaotic, but she never allowed Jim to enter it, and so he thought of it as filled with unguents and gauzy things. There were always guests, counts and duchesses and dukes, but they brought no possessions with them, and they bought none in Winnipeg.

It's hard to say if Jim was happy. By the time he'd figured out that getting what he wanted had nothing to do with happiness, it was too late. He died in his sleep one night. He awoke for a second with the feeling he was falling and a terrible sense that he had forgotten to do something important, and he snuffed out like a candle.

Leila stayed for the funeral, but by the weekend she had sold the penthouse and was gone. Each of his first two wives visited his grave once. Julia stole some flowers from a nearby grave and put them on Jim's. Susan brought some friends and they read a poem to cello music. She removed the wilted flowers and plucked out some of the quack grass.

Below them, Jim rested quietly. There was nothing in the coffin but him. He didn't have to do anything. There was no place to go. Whatever he needed, somebody else would have to pay for it.

FIFTH GAIT

he horses of Iceland have a fifth gait, the tölt. They can walk, trot, gallop and pace as well. When they use the tölt, only one leg at a time touches the ground, and the noise they make is a rapid tattoo. The gait is so smooth that you can drink a glass of whisky without spilling a drop. And the tölt can be faster than the gallop.

In 1983, I sat in a farmhouse in Iceland a few miles from the Arctic Circle, drinking scotch. A horizontal sun poured golden light into the room. A herd of Icelandic horses galloped by the window. The golden light caught in their flying manes, and for a moment, time paused and I could see every detail, the flecks of saliva on their mouths, the individual hairs of their coats, even the disturbance of the air they breathed. Then they thundered by. I was drinking scotch. I didn't spill a drop.

When Grettir Asmundson was made an outlaw, he lived on the island of Drangey. When his fire went out, he swam a full mile to the mainland, and then swam back with a basket full of coals. He didn't drop a single coal into the freezing arctic sea. So much is a matter of balance.

That was a long time ago, and when my grandfather told me the story, I thought it had happened in Canada, on the shores of Lake Winnipeg. I thought the island was Hecla Island. In 1993, I stood where Grettir had stood, and looked over to Drangey Island. I could never swim that far. At least I know that much.

The Icelandic horse is short, only about thirteen hands, but it is stocky and can carry a much heavier load than most horses. You may not call it a pony. It travels over the treeless, black, volcanic plains using the tölt, as smooth and seamless as a glass of scotch.

If you are climbing alone in the mountains, especially if you are a child, you must beware of Nökkur. He is the most beautiful of horses, and he wants you to ride him, but if you do, he will carry you off to a lake high in the mountains, and he will take you under that lake to where he lives. Everyone will think you have drowned. You can recognize him because his hoofs are on backwards.

About two hours north of Reykjavik, someone has restored an old sod farmhouse, though it looks not so much like something restored as like something that has always been there. Next door is a church. When I went to look at the church, a tourist doing what tourists do, there was a funeral going on. Several hundred people had gathered, more than the church could hold, and they milled around the building in their elegant dress. The next day we checked the obituary pages in the local paper. A great horseman had died. He had eight obituaries. The next day he had five and the third day he had four. A man of many friends.

My wife is out this very minute learning how to ride Icelandic horses. She came to riding late, and so takes it more seriously than a young girl might. She wants to get it right, and she takes lessons and studies books about the correct posture, about finding the right seat. She can walk, trot, gallop and pace, and now she is looking for the fifth gait, looking for perfect balance.

When I was a child, horses were everywhere. The T. Eaton

Company delivered its catalogue orders throughout Winnipeg in elegant blue carriages pulled by perfectly matched teams of horses. At my grandmother's farm, a herd of horses galloped dangerously through the yard every night just at dusk. They had been there when my grandfather died, and my grandmother continued to feed them for twenty years, though they were never harnessed. When she became ill and had to go to a nursing home, her sons caught them and sold them.

Once, on our way back from a glacier in Iceland, we were caught in a roundup of sheep. There was only one road, and we had to share it with hundreds of them, every shade available to sheep. Our Land Rover crawled by, directly into the setting sun. The sheep were being herded by young men on horseback. Every man had at least one child with him, blond and intense, sharing his saddle. The riders and horses were haloed by the light. Space explorers on a different planet couldn't have felt more alien than I did then.

I grew up with horses, but I never learned to love them. They were too large and too unpredictable, and my relationship with them was too formal. I had to harness them, hook their traces to the singletree of the rake or the doubletree of the hayrack and drive them out to the fields to work. I spent hours following Minnie and Betty, Princess and Tom. Sometimes, I would ride them, either to the fields or back, harnessed, usually, but sometimes bareback. I know I should have learned to care for them, but sometimes familiarity is not enough.

In California last winter, my wife went for a trail ride into a desert canyon. It was the first trip of the day, and she was the only customer. Her trail guide was a cowboy from Oklahoma. He was an Ian Tyson fan, and during the off-season he sang in bars in Los Angeles. He sang her love songs as they rode through the cacti and sand. He was leather-skinned and looked alcoholic, my wife told me. He showed her a cactus wren, but when she checked it later in the bird book, it was something else. And I could never hold a tune.

At the Moscow Circus, just before the failed coup when everything seemed possible, I watched an amazing narrative told entirely with men on horseback. The lights dimmed. The music came up. Something threatened a storm. A dozen riders swept into the ring, circling at an impossible speed. Suddenly at the edge of the ring a maiden was watching. The most daring of the riders plucked the red bandanna from his neck and threw it onto the ground. The next round, he leaned from his saddle and picked it up with his teeth. Then he picked up the girl and swept her onto his saddle behind him. They rode erotically in the gathering darkness of the ring until suddenly her brothers arrived, riding frantically and holding torches. Somehow, and I'm surprised that I can no longer remember how, the girl was killed and the brothers and the lover and his friends rode out to a sad funereal end.

The Icelandic saddle is different from either the English saddle or the western saddle. It is set further back on the horse for a different balance. It sets most of the weight over the back legs, and this, I am told, makes it easier for the horse to walk over the rough volcanic fields of the Icelandic interior. A horse with such a saddle can carry more weight than if saddled in the western way.

At Fort Steele, just outside Cranbrook, British Columbia, you can find the largest herd of black Clydesdales in the country. They are enormous, powerful horses, but the soft fall of white hair that covers their huge hoofs makes them somehow fragile, as if beauty were clumsily allied with strength.

My uncle was president of the Horseman's Benevolent Protective Association. He raised racehorses and ran them at the local racetrack. He always raised them from scratch rather than buying them. He liked to win, but since he always lost money, it couldn't have been winning that lured him to horse-racing. I asked him about this once, and he told me there's something about the outside of a horse that's good for the inside of a man.

Odin's horse was faster than the wind. He was named Sleipnir and he had eight legs. Odin rode him into battle, when he led the Valkyries to choose the bravest of warriors to die and join him in the festivities at Valhalla. His feet were on the right way.

Not long ago, we spent some time in New Zealand, driving from motel to motel in our little rented Ford, trying to figure out what the extravagant amount of roadkill might mean. What were all those dead animals? Were New Zealanders more dangerous than other drivers? In the month we were there, we never ran over anything ourselves.

And my wife did notice that whenever we saw horses in the fields they were invariably covered with blankets. And yet it was February, only the end of summer, and both the days and nights were warm. We asked many people about the problem but nobody knew the answer. Yes, they said, they knew that horses wore blankets, but it had never occurred to them they might not.

I went to watch my niece compete in the finals of the Pony Club competition for the Canadian championship. She had won it before and was considered the one to watch. The young girls who were competing looked awkward and coltish when they were not in costume and seated on their horses. Most of the mothers were stage mothers, investing their whole lives in their daughters' talents. I stood with the fathers, mostly overweight, distracted men with a lot of money who wanted to buy their daughters' dreams for them. My niece won again. When she rode, it was difficult to tell where the girl ended and the horse began.

For a couple of hours one September afternoon, I watched a horse roundup in a valley in the west of Iceland. From every direction, men on foot with dogs chased horses from high in the mountains down to a set of corrals at the centre of the valley. The horses were funnelled into a maze of fences and emerged in separate pastures where each horseman could gather his own. But I couldn't help wondering whether the herds from the mountains represented the same groupings of horses as the herds in the corrals. Had those horses, in the wildness of their summer, made new commitments, organized themselves into herds that served the interests of horses, not people? Was there something tragic in this separation? Some lack of balance?

In New Brunswick, I went to a heavy-horse hauling contest at Burtt's Corner. The horses were working farm horses, most of them part something, part Belgian, part Clydesdale, part Percheron. Men hitched the horses to a flatbed loaded with concrete blocks, then measured how far the team could pull before it came to a stop. I remember a man and his five-year-old son watching together. Their stances were identical, one foot forward, hip thrust sideways, cap pulled low over the eyes. Each had a large trucker's wallet in his back pocket and each was chewing on a straw. There was something odd in such perfect reproduction.

Iceland banned the entry of horses other than the Icelandic horse in 1100. For nine hundred years no other kind of horse has been permitted. An Icelandic horse who leaves the country may never return, though the Icelanders are less fussy about their citizens. But then, dogs and cats are not permitted in cities or towns, and until recently, there was no television on Thursdays.

I grow old. It gets harder to find a balance. I sleep too late or I do not sleep at all. The things I believe are not much in favour these days, and I find it hard to read a newspaper. My wife is in love with horses. My children are scattered and gone. The phone rings and I don't answer it. The mail piles up on my desk. I need a rapid tattoo, a tölt, a fifth gait, some way of moving smoothly and swiftly across the surface of my life, my glass so carefully balanced I never spill a drop.

ME AND ALEC WENT FISHING WITH RIMBAUD

e and Alec went fishing with Rimbaud. Rimbaud was drunk. He was singing an old Hank Snow number, "Movin' On," but he had a terrible French accent, and he wasn't much of a singer. I was in the back of the boat, running the motor, and Alec was up front with Rimbaud. Rimbaud kept putting his hand on Alec's knee and calling him My Little Pussycat, but Alec was too busy untying his fishing line to pay much attention. The motor kept catching fire, and I had to smother the flames with my nylon jacket.

Rimbaud and me were using pickerel rigs, but Alec ties his own flies. He makes lovely bluebottles out of black thread. He was dipping them into a little jar of garbage that he always carries with him, because, he says, the fish like the smell. Rimbaud didn't like the smell, and so he refused to sit with Alec. He wanted to sit in the back of the boat with me, but I didn't like the smell of Rimbaud, so I made him sit in the front. He got sulky and refused to talk, but a lot of nineteenth-century Frenchmen are like that, so I didn't worry too much.

We were drinking absinthe, passing around the bottle. You

can't get absinthe in the local liquor store, but Alec's brother from Duluth had sent him a bottle. He'd been saving it for a special occasion, but it was his turn to bring the bottle and that's all he had in the house. Rimbaud got over his sulking fit pretty soon, and was doing his imitation of Brenda Lee, only he got the words to "Jambalaya" mixed up with "Shrimp Boats Are A-Coming." He tried to kiss Alec on the neck, but Alec said, "Get away from me, you fag. Did you come out to fish or just to piss around?"

Rimbaud was miffed. "I'm a great tragic poet," he shouted. "I am red. See the laughter spill from my beautiful lips. Watch. I spit out blood. I don't have to take this treatment from you, you little turd."

He didn't actually spit blood, but it was pretty disgusting anyway. He'd been chewing Copenhagen, and he put a big brown gob on Alec's foot. Luckily, Alec didn't notice.

Now they were both sulking. The fish weren't biting anyway, so I tried to cheer them up with a couple of Polish jokes, but it didn't work. They both claimed that they had Polish grandmothers and said I'd affronted them. Rimbaud was trying to make up with Alec.

"You are green," he said, "a vibration of the divine seas, the peace of fresh meadows. Your great brow is furrowed with wrinkles."

"What do you mean wrinkles?" Alec asked, a little testily.

"Well, you have to admit, you've got a lot of wrinkles."

"I do not."

"You do so."

"Do not."

"All right, forget it then. I was just trying to be friendly."

"Okay, but no more poetry. You're scaring the fish."

Rimbaud seemed to be satisfied with the new arrangement and he started humming "Jailhouse Rock." The motor caught fire again and I was a little worried. I'd burned up most of my nylon jacket already, and I wasn't sure there was enough left to smother the flames. I managed to get it out, though, and when I turned around, Alec and Rimbaud were playing chess with a little magnetic chessboard that Rimbaud had in his pocket. They were quarrelling again. Rimbaud accused Alec of stealing the white king.

"There was no white king, you silly bugger," Alec told him.

Rimbaud fixed Alec with a glacial stare. "Enough farting around, Alec," he said. "Let's be perfectly candid about this. You're jealous because I'm a great poet and you're just a little nobody, and so you've stolen my white king out of spite."

"Screw you."

Rimbaud leered. "That's a wonderful idea. But let's finish this game of chess first."

"It's finished," Alec said. "You've lost your king, so I win. That's the rules."

"That's not fair," Rimbaud shouted. "You've got to capture him."

"I did," Alec said, pulling the piece out of his shirt pocket. "I captured him while you were vomiting over the side of the boat." He passed the white king back to Rimbaud, who seemed a little bad-tempered about the whole business.

For a little while everybody just fished. I caught a couple of saugers, and Alec caught two perch and a sunfish. Rimbaud caught a tiny bullhead using a fly that Alec had given him, and refused to throw it back. I told him they were no good to eat, but he said it looked sensitive, and he couldn't bear the thought of it having to live in that dirty water. Then he threw Alec's sunfish back, because, he said, it was too ugly. Alec was pissed off because his father-in-law loves sunfish and he was going to give the fish to him. He refused to give Rimbaud any more flies, so Rimbaud had to use my minnows.

Rimbaud was singing an old Platter's number, "The Great Pretender," and he was trying to do the backup stuff too. Alec asked me to make him stop, but he was Alec's friend, not mine. Besides, I was having trouble with the motor again. It's an old ten-horse Johnson with the gas tank built in, and you know how temperamental those things are. I took out the spark plug and dried it with a match. The motor chugged a couple of times and then finally started and I headed for shore, because it had started to rain. Rimbaud and Alec were arguing again, but I couldn't make out what they were saying over the noise of the motor. Rimbaud had Alec's pocket knife and was threatening to commit suicide by driving it into his heart. Alec seemed to be telling him to go ahead. I screamed at them to sit down in the boat. Lake Winnipeg is dangerous enough without having a couple of poets fighting in your boat. Maybe I didn't tell you, but Alec is also a poet. Or at least he claims to be. He runs off his books on a little mimeograph machine he bought from the church when they got a Xerox. I can't make head nor tail of his writing. Anyway, that's how he met Rimbaud, at one of those poet's things.

When we got back to the dock, it was eleven o'clock, and Rimbaud wanted to go to the pub. I didn't think it was a good idea, because we were drunk enough. We'd finished the entire bottle of absinthe. Alec thought maybe we could pick up some girls, but I told him I didn't want any girl you could pick up at the pub at eleven o'clock in the morning. Rimbaud didn't want any girls either. He wanted Alec, but Alec told him to forget it. Rimbaud got sulky again, so we decided to go to the pub after all to cheer him up. When we got to the pub, Rimbaud was singing "That's Amore" and doing a pretty good imitation of Dean Martin. I told him he'd have to stop, because they don't allow singing in the pub. He said great poets could sing wherever they wanted. Alec threatened to break his fingers if he didn't stop. Alec and Rimbaud each ordered a mug of draft, and I had a Miller Highlife. You didn't used to be able to get it, and I wanted to see what it was like. It tasted pretty much the same as any domestic beer.

We had quite a few bottles, and Alec and Rimbaud got into a big argument over poetry. Rimbaud claimed that the vowels were different colours, but Alec said that this was just a figure of speech. Rimbaud claimed that he could actually see the colours, and by that time he was so drunk he probably could. I was thinking about Alice Simpson, who lives over in South Beach. Her husband left her with two little kids, and she's on welfare. She's really a good girl, but I figured if I took over a bottle of gin, after a while maybe she wouldn't be so good. You know how it is when you get drunk. You get crazy ideas, but sometimes they work out.

Rimbaud had just moved over to Big Jim Maloney's table and was telling Big Jim lies about all the fish we had caught. He had his hand on Big Jim's knee and was practically whispering in his ear. Big Jim didn't seem to mind, so you never can tell. Or maybe he'd never met anyone like Rimbaud, so he didn't know what was going on. If that was the case, there was going to be hell to pay when Big Jim figured it out. Alec was muttering something, but when I asked him what he had said, he told me he was singing an old Italian folk song that his mother had taught him.

I told Alec that I'd pick him up at five a.m. next Saturday to go fishing, but he couldn't bring any poets along. He said he'd promised some guy named D'Annunzio, but I said no way, no more poets. Painters or sculptors are fine because they keep their mouths shut, but poets are no good because they are always talking, and you lose your concentration and maybe you don't notice a nibble. Then I bought a mickey of gin and went over to Alice Simpson's place and that worked out just fine.

In The Garden
of the Medicis

oe slowed the Toyota and pulled over to the edge of the road. They seemed to have been climbing for a very long time, the Toyota unable to handle the steep grade in anything higher than third gear. Now steam billowed from the engine. Carla turned her attention to the children in the back seat.

"It's okay," she told them. "Daddy will get it fixed in a minute. Just stay still and don't undo your seat belts."

"Daddy's not going to get us out of this one so easy," Joe muttered under his breath, but he only said, "Oh, nothing" when Carla asked what he'd said.

Joe opened the hood of the car and looked at the motor. Steam was still coming from around the radiator cap, but it seemed to have slowed down a bit. A Jeep came from the opposite direction, but it passed without even slowing down, and Joe realized that they hadn't seen any other cars for a quite a while.

Water, he thought. I'll have to get some water to fill up the radiator, then maybe we can limp to a garage.

But there was no water anywhere near, no ditch, no mountain stream, not even a puddle. There were only the high banks of the rock cut on both sides and a few small rocks that had tumbled onto the road.

"Nothing I can do," Joe told Carla. "We've boiled over. I have to add antifreeze, or at least water, before we can drive anywhere."

"Didn't we pass a garage a while back?" Carla asked. "Or a motel or something? Someplace that might at least have a phone?"

"I don't know," Joe said. "We passed something, but it might have been twenty miles away."

"You can just glide down the hill," Jason said from the back seat. He was eleven and had just recently felt old enough to offer advice to adults. "Just turn around and we'll keep on gliding until we find something."

"Oh, sure," Kerry, his older sister, needled him. "And the brakes will fail and we'll go off the side of a cliff. Besides, we've got power steering and power brakes. Neither of those things works unless the motor is running."

After a half-hour, in which only one vehicle passed, a bus whose passengers apparently thought his appeal for help was simple friendliness and waved at him from the window, Joe was prepared to follow Jason's advice.

"Sure," Kerry said. "Now we'll all die."

"Enough," her mother told her, and that quieted her. Kerry was fifteen and given to unexplained moments of weeping, as if she had suffered some great tragedy but was forbidden to speak of it.

Joe cranked the wheel of the Toyota, and it was much easier to push than he had thought it would be. It also started downhill much faster than he'd expected, and if Carla hadn't pulled on the emergency brake, he would have been left behind watching his family rocket to their fates.

"I'm going to go quite slowly," Joe told the family. "Look for signs. Sometimes there are places that you don't notice until the last second."

And it happened in that way. They had drifted slowly downward for about five minutes when Carla saw a small sign that would have been unreadable to anyone going faster than five miles an hour. It read Garden of the Medicis and it marked an almost invisible road that led steeply down. Joe turned without hesitation, and the Toyota bounced over the uneven gravel path. There were hairpin bends he could hardly negotiate and, before long, the brakes were beginning to smell.

There better be something at the bottom, Joe thought to himself, or we'll never get out of here. All that stood between his family and starvation was a couple of Cokes and a large bag of tortilla chips.

There *was* something at the bottom. A stunning mountain lake that appeared to be half blue and half green with a blur of pink in the centre. They caught glimpses of it through the trees, and, just as they made the final turn, it opened before them in all its glory.

"Wow," Kerry said. "No boats, no cottages, no anything. Just water and sand." The Toyota eased to a final stop just at the very edge of a large sandy beach.

"At least there's water," Joe said. "I can probably get the car started, though I don't know if we'll ever climb out of here without boiling over again."

They all got out to look at the lake, and Jason discovered another sign that said Garden of the Medicis with an arrow that pointed down a narrow path along the shore.

"We may as well find out what it is," Carla said, and they walked single file through the ferns and shrubs that surrounded the pathway. After just a minute of walking, they rounded a little headland and came on another bay and sandy beach. Here, a garish pink building with a false front and a high fence proclaimed itself the Garden of the Medicis in ornate lettering. A string of coloured lights hung just above the fence, and a gate that was framed with pillars so that it looked ancient and Roman was locked with a padlock. The windows of the main building were boarded over, and though a sign on the door said Open, the building was locked.

Joe rapped on the door, but there was no answer. He rapped again, and a voice from behind them said, "No use knocking. It's closed."

The voice came from a young man of indeterminate age. He might have been in his early twenties, but he might also have been much younger. He wore shorts and a white T-shirt with a baseball cap turned backwards. He was barefoot.

"What is this place?" Jason asked. He seemed to have decided in favour of the man's youth, and there was nothing of awe or respect in his voice.

The young man didn't answer for a while. His eyes were a startling green. "It's a resort," he said finally. "Or at least it used to be. It's been closed for years. I'm the caretaker." Then, as if he had decided that they posed no threat, he confided, "It's just a summer job. I watch that nobody vandalizes the place or sets it on fire or anything. Apparently it was really popular around the time of the First World War, but it's been closed for about seventy years." Joe turned back to the building. He noticed that what he had first thought was a decorative motif on the pillars of the gate was actually real grape leaves.

The young man's name was Tomaso, and he was working his way through university. He didn't really know much about the place. He'd answered an ad in the newspaper, and the next thing he knew, he was here. Once a week, a truck came by and left him supplies, but the rest of the time, he just read the novels he had brought with him. He helped Joe fill up the radiator with water and waved goodbye as they started up the hill.

About a hundred yards further, the steam from the engine made it impossible to see at all. This time Joe noticed the hole in the hose from which the steam issued. Tomaso could think of no solution. He had no phone, and the truck did not come until Thursday, another four days. He had plenty of food, though, and if they wanted to camp, he'd be glad to help out. The kids loved the idea, and even Carla seemed content.

"You wanted something unspoiled," she said. "You're not going to get much better than this."

They set up their tent back on the first little bay near the car. The kids wanted to set up by the Garden of the Medicis where Tomaso had his tent, but Joe had noticed a bit too much eagerness on Kerry's part, and he wasn't prepared to be caught in the middle of the fantasy of a summer's romance. She was certain to fall in love with Tomaso, and then she'd weep all the way to Vancouver when they left.

Tomaso brought over a bunch of wieners and stale buns, and they ate hot dogs. Joe took out a couple of lawn chairs, and he and Carla read in the shade of an old ponderosa pine. Tomaso and the kids went swimming, Kerry in a bikini, which Joe would certainly have banned if he had seen it before that moment. Then the sun slipped behind a mountain, and though it was only four o'clock, the air was suddenly cold.

Tomaso brought cans of ravioli, and they cooked it in a frying pan over an open fire. Everybody agreed it was one of the finest meals they had ever eaten. Finally, Tomaso said good night and disappeared into the path along the edge of the lake. He'd be back with breakfast, he said.

Sometime in the night, Joe awoke to the faint sound of music. When he got out of the tent, he could no longer hear it. The night was starry and clear, and the lake was entirely silver. Joe walked to the edge of the lake, and dipped his toe. To his surprise, the lake was warm. On an impulse, he slipped off his pyjama bottoms and waded in. The water was as soft and pure as silk. It got deep quickly, but it seemed to have more buoyancy than water should have. Joe had never thought of himself as a good swimmer, but now he moved with ease, slicing his way through the water.

He aimed for the point of land that separated the Garden of the Medicis from the campsite. It was a long swim for him, but he wasn't far from shore, and he could always return along the beach. He rolled over and eased into a gentle backstroke. He felt he could go on for hours. When he thought he must be past the point, he rolled over to see the shore brilliantly lit by hanging lanterns. A shape loomed out of the lake in front of him, and as it passed, he realized it was a gondola, a dark figure in a striped shirt poling it, and lovers clasped in each other's arms at the far end. The music was unmistakable now. Figures flitted along the beach, and he could hear the ripple of laughter above the music. He could make out other craft now, and a barge, brightly lit and decorated with flowers, was anchored in the centre of the bay.

Joe swam in to the shore. As soon as he left the water, he was intensely conscious that he was naked, so he kept very close to the line of trees. A couple came down the beach, and he hid behind a tree as they passed. The man was wearing an elegant three-piece suit with a striped tie and a white shirt, but he was barefoot. The tie-pin and cufflinks gleamed against the darkness of the lake. The woman wore a long white gown and a tiara. She, too, was barefoot. They stopped directly in front of Joe, and the man took the woman in his arms.

"It'll be over in three months," the man told the woman. "That's what everybody says. If I don't go, how will I ever live with myself later?"

"Just don't get yourself killed," the woman said. "They say the Ramsay boy got killed in France a couple of weeks ago."

"I won't get killed," the man said. "Three months. That's a promise." And he folded her in his arms and kissed her. Joe thought the woman was the most beautiful person he had ever seen, and he felt embarrassed at witnessing the intimacy before him. He found the path just back of the beach and continued down it to the Garden of the Medicis. The building was ablaze with light, and dozens of teams of horses still hitched to elegant coaches and wagons stamped their hoofs and whinnied on the night air.

Joe edged his way to the beginning of the fence, then plunged into the undergrowth and followed the line of the fence to a spot where he could climb the low branches of a tree and see over.

Inside was what seemed the balcony of a ballroom. Through a set of open doors, Joe could see dancers whirling to the music of an orchestra. Women with fans cooled themselves behind the pillars of the balcony. Joe listened intently to hear what they were saying, but all he could make out was "The Count. The Count."

Then a man dressed in an elaborate costume that looked like something from a Shakespearean play appeared, accompanied by a tall elegant woman in a jewelled gown. The woman looked amazingly like Carla. Her hair was swept up in an elaborate coiffure that showed off the lines of her neck. A small page in a black uniform with ruffled sleeves brought them glasses of wine on a silver tray. The page looked remarkably like Jason. Joe wished he could get closer, but any further movement would reveal him naked to the dancers.

"Anything you wish, my dear," the Count said. "But it must look like an accident. We shall report him as drowned." These words came sharply and clearly, but it was impossible to hear what the woman answered. The count and the woman followed the page back into the ballroom.

For a while there was no one, only the whirl of distant dancers and the music. Then a young couple emerged from a doorway below the balcony. Joe had not noticed it before. They were laughing, and the young man tried to kiss the woman, who twisted away and ran towards the fence where Joe was hiding. In the light from a lantern, their faces were clear. The young woman was Kerry and the man was Tomaso. He was dressed entirely in black and she in a wispy white dress. He caught her just below the branches of Joe's tree and this time she did not resist his kiss.

"Kerry," Joe shouted. "What are you doing?"

The lovers looked up at the tree and discovered Joe there in all his nakedness. The woman he had thought was Kerry screamed, and in a moment the lawn in front of the balcony was filled with running figures. Joe slipped out of the tree and made his way back through the undergrowth, not daring to walk either on the path or on the beach. Branches whipped into his eyes, and he stepped on sharp roots and stones. There were cobwebs everywhere.

Finally, he made it back to the campsite. He picked up his pyjama bottoms where he had let them fall by the lake, and he put them on. He checked the kids' tent. Kerry and Jason were both sound asleep in their sleeping bags. Carla snored gently in the larger tent. Joe rummaged through his suitcase and found the half bottle of rye he kept there, and he took a long draw directly from the bottle.

The next morning, Tomaso arrived with breakfast, Aunt Jemima pancake mix and some emergency powdered eggs. Joe asked him if he had heard anything odd last night. Tomaso had. Something, probably a bear, had been crashing around in the underbrush. He'd gone out to check and saw what looked like a naked man, though of course that was impossible. Some trick of the moonlight.

After breakfast, Joe asked Tomaso if they could look inside the Garden of the Medicis.

"I'm not supposed to," Tomaso said. "That's the one rule. I mustn't let anyone in or else I get fired. Besides, there's nothing there to see. Only a few old models in costumes and some ratty furniture. There's a window around the back you can see through if you want, but even I am not allowed to go in there."

By early afternoon, Carla had decided to take a nap, Jason was building a fort, and Tomaso was watching Kerry in her bikini, and not likely to move until she gave up swimming. Joe took a pail from the car and announced he was going to pick huckleberries. Nobody paid any attention to him.

The window around the back was just where Tomaso had said it was. Through the window, Joe could make out tattered furniture and obscure figures in the shadows. The window was locked with a small clasp. Joe took out his Swiss army knife and twisted the clasp. The wood was rotten, and the clasp came out easily. Joe put it in his pocket and crawled through the window into the shadowy room.

The room was apparently a storeroom. Old flowered sofas were piled on top of each other, but they were covered with sheets and appeared to be in better shape than the dust and cobwebs would lead you to expect. Chairs were piled haphazardly, and all along one side of the room costumes hung from hooks on the wall. Like the sofas, the costumes were protected by sheets, and were in much better condition than Joe had expected. He took down a brown three-piece suit that looked like the one the barefoot man on the beach had worn, and tried the jacket on. It fit him perfectly. A batch of parasols stood upside down in an elephant's-foot basket. Ornate gilt mirrors and lamps were propped between the other items.

The figures that Tomaso had mentioned were gathered near a staircase that led upwards. They appeared to be made from papier-mâché, and much of the paint had chipped from them. There were six figures in all, and they represented the serving classes: a cook, a waiter, two maids, a pageboy and a butler. It seemed that the Garden of the Medicis had once been a museum. The top of the stairway was much brighter than the room below, as if it were lit by electric lights.

It was sunlight that lit the room, Joe discovered when he entered it. The stairway led to the ballroom he had seen from his tree the night before. The ballroom was much larger than seemed possible when you looked at the building from outside. Here, figures were gathered in groups. The musicians, complete with instruments, were frozen in mid-song at the far end of the room. Couples swooped and dipped in an elaborate minuet. These figures were far better made than the ones below. They were exquisitely shaped from some material that Joe could not identify. At first glance it looked like wax, but the surface, when you touched it, had all the softness of skin. There was not a speck of dust or a cobweb anywhere.

The Count and the woman Joe had seen with him the night before stood in the opening of the balcony. Seen more closely, the female figure's resemblance to Carla was superficial. It was about the same size with the same colour hair, but the eyes were different. The small page who presented them with wine did look like Jason, but only in the way that an army of small boys in uniform would resemble each other. The expression on the Count's face seemed to be rage. His eyes followed Joe in an eerie way as Joe moved about the room.

From the balcony, Joe could see the tree in which he had hidden the night before. His hiding-place in daylight was obvious, impossible to miss. On the lawn, the figure he had taken to be Tomaso chased Kerry's double in a parody of young love. In a dimmer light, it might be possible to mistake them for the real thing.

Joe was about to leave when he noticed a door behind the musicians, leading to an alcove. He slipped behind the curtains that separated the musicians from the room, and entered. There the beautiful woman he had seen on the beach leaned in a gesture of mourning and grief over a figure who lay on a hospital bed. The figure was dressed in full military uniform, but his chest was covered with blood, and an open hole showed that he had been shot through the heart.

Joe leaned over to see whether the figure was the one he had seen on the beach, the man who had promised to return in three months. It was like looking into a mirror. The face that stared up at him was clearly his own.

On his way back to the camp, Joe decided to confront Tomaso. Tomaso obviously knew more than he had let on. Someone tended those figures daily. Someone vacuumed the dust and the cobwebs, and polished the instruments of the musicians. On an impulse, he turned back and examined the earth in front of the Garden of the Medicis. The prints of horses were everywhere, and the tracks of wagons led up a path into the forest.

Tomaso was not there when Joe arrived. He had told the children that part of his duties included checking on a cabin on the other side of the lake, and he had taken a canoe and paddled off. He had offered to take Kerry for a ride, but Carla had vetoed that plan, and now Kerry was weeping gently in the tent.

"There are no ripe huckleberries yet," Joe told Carla, but he didn't tell her about his visit to the Garden of the Medicis.

"At nine o'clock tomorrow morning the truck comes with the supplies," Carla told him. "Then we can get away from here. It's beautiful and everything, but there's something very strange about this place. I don't think I like it."

Tomaso did not come back with supper, as he had promised,

and everyone was a little hungry and a little cranky by dark. Kerry was certain that Tomaso had drowned, and wanted to set out to rescue him. Joe explained that there was no way to rescue him since they had no boat, and Kerry went back to the tent and wept some more.

When the music started that night, Joe vowed to resist it. By nine the next morning, they would be gone, and whatever ghosts inhabited the Garden of the Medicis could go on without him. But the image of the woman looking down at his own dead body haunted him, and he couldn't sleep. He rolled over to put his arm around Carla, seeking comfort, but she was gone. Her sleeping bag was empty. He would probably find her, unable to sleep, sitting on a rock near the beach. He would tell her about the Garden of the Medicis.

But she was not on a rock near the beach. She was nowhere to be found. He looked into the kids' tent on the off chance that one of them was sick and she had gone to comfort them and fallen asleep. The kids' tent, too, was empty. He called their names into the darkness, but no one answered. The distant sound of violins drifted around the point.

Joe put on his bathing suit and walked down to the edge of the water. There was no moonlight, but the stars alone made the lake bright. The water was warm and as smooth as silk. Joe swam steadily until he rounded the point. The scene was nearly identical to what he had seen the other night. Boats flitted back and forth across the water, and people partied on a barge anchored in the bay. Joe swam to land right at the point and made his way along the beach to the brilliantly lit building at the centre of the bay. He heard the whinny of a horse and knew that the carriages were waiting in front. He crept along the fence until he reached the window he had pried open earlier. It swung open now with only the slightest creak.

The light pouring down the staircase from above made the room brighter than it had been during the day. Joe found the three-piece suit he had tried on earlier, and he put it on now. It fit perfectly, and once he had put on the white shirt, the tie, the tie-pin and the cufflinks, he thought he must be indistinguishable from the man he had seen on the beach. He couldn't find any shoes, but he consoled himself that the other man had also been barefoot.

Joe took a deep breath and walked up the stairs into the ballroom. The dancers swirled around so that he had to move back to the wall to avoid being hit. They were dressed in a strange assortment of costumes. Many of the women wore elaborate gowns, but some wore simple pleated white skirts and light sweaters. Flappers, Joe thought. That's what the costume was. Some of the men were dressed as courtiers, but most were in suits very much like Joe's own. Several wore army uniforms.

Joe made his way around the ballroom until he came to the balcony. The Count was standing with his back to the railing, talking to a tall blonde woman.

"It's settled," the Count told her. "Tonight's the night. And it will be perceived as a drowning."

"But won't there be an investigation?" she asked.

"They may investigate all they want," the Count replied. "There will be nothing here for them to investigate."

Just then a small page brought them each a glass of wine. He handed them the wine on a silver platter, then turned and walked right past Joe into the ballroom. The page was Jason. There was no doubt about it. He looked directly into his father's eyes but gave no hint of recognition.

The Count and the woman turned to go back into the ballroom, and the woman was certainly Carla. In the afternoon, when her features had been frozen, it had been difficult to tell, but now there was no doubt. As soon as they had left the balcony, Joe walked to the railing and looked over. A young couple were in a tight embrace under the tree in which he had sat naked the other night. They pulled apart reluctantly, and in the light that poured from a window he identified them positively. Kerry and Tomaso.

Joe thought he should do something, but there didn't seem to be anything he could do. The music surged and the dancers whirled. From one window, he could see the boats on the lake and the lights from the barge. He moved past the musicians to the alcove where he had seen the woman and the representation of himself, but it was empty. From the window, he could see the teams of horses in front, and a little higher up the bank, Tomaso's tent.

Suddenly, a woman was in his arms. The woman from the beach who had mourned him that very day.

"You're alive," she said. "I saw you dead only a few hours ago, but you're alive."

"No," Joe said. "It's all a mistake." But the woman silenced him with her lips, and he kissed her back, a long, slow, delirious kiss. Then she moved back a little so that she was staring into his face.

"Let me look at you," she said.

Joe looked back at her, but over her shoulder he could see Tomaso's tent and the horses and drivers. People were beginning to leave the Garden of the Medicis and climb into the carriages. One by one, they drove off into the darkness. Then the sun came over the mountain and Tomaso came out of his tent. He stretched languidly and walked out of sight as if to meet someone. In a moment he was back, and a truck towed Joe's Toyota into the clearing. Tomaso and the other man did something under the hood, then Tomaso started the car. Carla appeared then, and from a distance, it looked as if she had been weeping. Jason climbed into the back seat of the car, and Kerry walked over to Tomaso and kissed him a gentle goodbye kiss. Joe could hear their voices, but the only word he could make out was "drowned."

Then a man in a bathing suit rushed into the clearing and Carla flung herself into his arms. Joe couldn't be sure, but it looked like the man he had seen barefoot on the beach. He wished he could move closer to the window, but the woman in his arms was motionless and he didn't dare disturb her. The man in the bathing suit got into the car, and it followed the truck up the pathway the horses had used the night before.

The road up the mountain was even steeper than the road down. The Toyota choked, and the man driving was afraid it might start to boil over again, but after a minute it seemed like the repair was going to work. The children were silent in the back seat.

"You know something?" the man in the driver's seat said, and then he hesitated.

"What?"

"Never mind," he said. He was sure there was something he had to tell his wife. He felt that something terribly important had happened at the Garden of the Medicis, something that would change everything, but he couldn't quite remember what it was. They rounded a bend and popped out onto the highway. He turned on the radio and the car filled with the sound of violins.

TORCH SONG

ne of the most attractive things about women is their awkardness, the sense they often give of not being entirely in control of their bodies. You catch it sometimes when they are opening doors or lighting a cigarette, that sense that they might stumble and fall. It is true even of athletes and dancers, perhaps especially true of them.

The choreographer is tall and slim, elegant in a Gallic way, with a small, neat moustache. There is nothing effeminate about him. He listens to the music twice, paying no apparent attention, then moves to the ramp. He signals the piano player to begin. With the slightest hitch of his body, he adopts a pose so provocatively female that the lounging actors laugh with embarrassment. He sings the first few bars of the song, rolling the feather boa sensously up his body, then spins, rolls his shoulder, makes a motion that seems impossible for a man, and ends in a posture that makes him seem to pout, though there is no expression on his face.

The actress is beside him. When he calls for the piano to begin again, she imitates the moves, but it is all wrong. She is too much herself, too much the woman poised to fall. On her, the stage gestures seem like excess clothing. The smooth eroticism of the choreographer's dance is mocked by the intense sense we onlookers have of her body, by her own sense of her body. Her hands are wrong. The choreographer strokes himself, arches and curves hand and wrist in a gesture we hadn't known before to be sexual. Her lost hands flutter in confusion, but her face is intense, her eyes are fixed on him.

For a few minutes they repeat this fragment of dance, mover and shadow. Then the choreographer is off the stage, muttering something to the director, who takes notes. The actress is immobilized on the stage, her eyes cast down like a slave at auction. The actors lose interest. They roll their heads back, close their eyes and mutter their scripts in a rapid half-whisper. The piano player invents a riff, likes it and impro- vises something that is clearly a beginning, an invitation to enter.

Then, the choreographer signals the piano player again, a half-wave, the palm upward. The actress begins. She has hardly made her first step before the choreographer has stopped the music. The arm is wrong. It must shape a delicate arabesque in the air. They begin again, and this time she gets it right. She flashes a smile at the piano player. Seven, eight, ten times she repeats the sequence, and each time there is less of her on the stage, more of the ghost of that motion the choreographer can step in and out of at will. He nods that it will do, and goes over to the stage manager. Together they consult a blueprint as if it were easier to understand the world in two dimensions than in three. The piano player takes a butter tart from a brown paper bag and begins to eat it. The actress whirls through her motions without the music, singing softly to herself and moving in a dream.

The dance is a series of strategies: how do you get from here to there? Each section is a detailed pattern of steps, a set of sinuous snakings of the body. The choreographer charges it with sexuality, as if female attractiveness were a set of abstract principles, as knowable as geometry. Each tiny series of movements is repeated a dozen times before moving to the next. With each new pattern, the actress grows in confidence, her body no longer the external manifestation of self, but something outside, to be moulded and moved. Even the Japanese fish, an erotic raising of the buttocks, is done without self-consciousness.

The choreographer seems unaware of her new sureness. No detail escapes him, no position of the foot, curve of the arm, goes uncorrected. He will allow no movement to the next step until the previous is perfect. The writers in the corner are arguing in low passionate terms, impervious to the glares of the actors trying to memorize their scripts. The choreographer leads the actress through her final flourish, the boa trailing into where there will be darkness.

It is time to run it through from the top. It seems perfect. The actress is brassy, salacious, full of energy. But no. The choreographer has found a dozen faults. She must walk through it slowly, without the music. Until now she has been dutiful, obedient, but now we begin to sense rebellion. Still, she says nothing, does what she is told. When she dances the number again, it is smoother but colder, the mind further from the body. With each repitition she is more graceful, the sequences becoming one.

Then it is lunch break. Three hours have passed and we have hardly noticed. The choreographer is brisk, official. He will be back in a week. At the Continental Lunch Bar we all order fish and chips again. We are full of banter, comic insults, making agreements behind the director's back. Only the actress does not join in. She is dreamy and preoccupied, as if she had just discovered some special knowledge. We are all as kind to her as we would be to an invalid, but she doesn't notice. Perhaps she is only trying to remember her steps, but on our way back to the theatre, she catches snowflakes with her tongue.

SOUTHERN CROSS

he dogs howled all night. Their din was a comfort to Michael. They reminded him that he was alive. Sarah slept beside him, a heavy lump in the bed. The neighbour's motion-sensor light came on every few minutes, a skunk or a rabbit, or maybe only the leaves on a willow rustling in the breeze that had blown from the south for days now.

A south wind meant low water. Not that it mattered. He hadn't been out on the lake for a dozen years, but he couldn't help searching the sky for signs. He was irrationally happy when the fishing was good.

Now he lurched out of bed and down the hall to the bathroom. His ankles and his knees betrayed him, full of pain. He thought he might fall, but he didn't. His tongue was thick, the taste in his mouth metallic, a sure sign that he had drunk too much. He urinated loudly into the centre of the bowl, shook carefully so as not to dribble onto the floor. The old man's trick, dribbling incontinently, and he wasn't ready for that yet.

The red light on the television in the bedroom had said five o'clock, too early to get up, but not much chance for more sleep. He opened the medicine cabinet and extracted an aspirin from the bottle. Sometimes that worked, and if it didn't help the hangover, at least it was an investment in avoiding a heart attack. As an afterthought, he also chewed a Tums, not because he actually needed one, but as a hedge against indigestion when he got back to bed.

He had turned out the light and was almost into bed before it hit him. Billy had cancer. Forty-four years old, and he was going to die in a stupid, humiliating way. Billy had told him just a few hours ago. As if it were something he had to apologize for, something that had happened as a result of an oversight or carelessness. It was already in his lungs and his liver. The doctor had recommended against even bothering with chemotherapy.

"I haven't got anybody," Billy said the next day over beer. "I'm going to leave it all to you." Then, as he realized there wasn't actually very much, he added, "Such as it is."

"Shit, Billy, don't talk like that," Michael said. "This has all got to be some sort of mistake. You're only forty-four."

"As soon as you're born, you're old enough to die," Billy said. "They're giving me six months, but the doctor admitted that I'd be lucky to make three. And the damnedest thing is, I still feel fine."

"Billy, you're not going to die," Michael said. "The world is a shitty place, but it's not that shitty."

"Australia," Billy said. "I always wanted to go to Australia."

"Well, go," Michael said. "Don't leave anybody any money. Take it and go to Australia."

"It don't work that way," Billy said. "There isn't any money till I die. It's all insurance. I got to be dead for anybody to get at that money, so you got to go for me."

There was thirty thousand dollars in insurance and Billy's Dodge van, which was actually worth nearly as much, and was also insured so that when he died it was all paid up. Billy died fast, but he died in horrible pain. At the end, he could only speak in whispers, and when Michael answered in a whisper, Billy told him to smarten up.

At the end, Billy would talk about nothing but Australia. He seemed to have an enormous amount of information about the country. "You go to Fiji on the way, and then you spend a couple of weeks in New Zealand," he said. "Then you fly to Tasmania, and you work your way north, up to Cairns and the Daintree Forest. You got to go see the Cathedral Fig Tree."

Billy didn't seem to realize that he was actually going to die, or else he didn't quite know what it meant. He seemed to think that after he was dead and Michael had gone to Australia, they would get together and talk about it. "The Ulysses butterflies," he'd say. "Great big buggers, so blue you can't even imagine it. I can hardly wait." And in the end, he went to die with some cousin in Brandon, and Michael wasn't there to see him through.

Sarah didn't want to go. "We can use the money for a house," she said. "I got my job at the hospital. If I quit, I'll never get another job like that."

"This isn't a choice," Michael told her. "We didn't get the money to buy a house. We got the money to go to Australia. If we don't go, I'll just flush it down the toilet."

But it wasn't as easy as that. Sarah dug in her heels and refused to go. She didn't even like the idea of Australia. If Michael wanted to go, he could have a divorce, but she wasn't budging.

And whoever was bluffing lost. Michael found himself with his separation papers in his pocket along with the ticket to Australia. He hadn't travelled much, once to Toronto on a chance of getting a job in Windsor that didn't work out, and another time to Calgary when his team won the provincial mixed curling. Now he stood in the airport in Nadi talking to a drunken engineer who thought they should get a place together in Suva.

"Sorry," Michael told him. "I've already booked a place down along the Coral Coast." And he went off to meet the mini-bus that would take him to the Fijian beaches, where the pictures showed surf riding in on silver sand.

Along the way, children in uniforms waited for buses,

young girls in brown or blue dresses with yellow or red scarves. Young boys in suits with caps. There were palm trees everywhere, curving trees with fronds, and giant ferns at the side of the road. The houses were mostly shacks, and old men and women shuffled in their yards, although it was still only seven in the morning.

The hotel was like something out of a fairy tale, but a Japanese fairy tale. There were silver beaches and stunning waves and palm trees and slow-moving Polynesians saying *bulu* all the time, but everyone there was Japanese except for two Australian couples, and Michael was too shy to speak to them. He spent a week in silence except for replying *bulu* to the help and describing the meal he would eat.

New Zealand was better, but Michael still couldn't enter things. The people were friendly and the country was beautiful, but he was going to Australia and he didn't want to take any chances with New Zealand. It was like being married and having a beautiful woman invite you up to her place for coffee. You wanted to go, but something told you it would be a mistake. He remembered the separation papers in his pocket, but they didn't help. It was Australia or nothing.

He rented a car and drove around the Coromandel Peninsula, then up to Rotorua and down to Wellington. He got to Wellington six days early, and he rented a motel as close to the airport as he could. Then he found a spot on the beach where a sign warned that penguins were crossing. He sat there all day for six days, but he never saw a single penguin. Maybe it was the wrong season.

It was raining when his plane pulled into Hobart. Nobody in the airport seemed to know who they were waiting for. They all held signs that read Auntie Mabel, or George Day, or Bishop Andrews. Michael was tempted to claim an identity and have his hand shaken and be ushered out into a waiting car and driven to a meeting of the synod or a family reunion or an early morning business briefing. But he took a taxi instead and went to the Sheraton Hotel overlooking the harbour. In the little magazine shop, he heard a voice that sounded Canadian asking for Tums, but he walked away before he saw who owned it.

That night, he sat in his room drinking scotch and looking over the harbour. A liner had drifted in at dusk, and it was all lit up and reflected in the water of the harbour. Michael tried to count the lights and estimate how many people were on it. A small town, he figured, and not such a small one at that.

The next day was a Saturday, and he could see the people from the liner massing inside a fenced-off area and moving through a set of gates. Beyond them were the tops of tents and an array of colours that suggested celebration. A circus, he guessed.

It was not a circus, but the Salamanca market, they informed him at the hotel desk. A bellboy or something, a man who seemed in charge and wore a label saying something in French, directed him to the market. It was only a couple of blocks away.

The market was a thriving collection of people selling the kinds of things you found in flea markets, leather and wood and possibly antique pottery, sandals and stuffed animals in the shape of kangaroos and Tasmanian devils. At the centre was a group of Vietnamese gardeners with wonderful vegetables and strange carved wooden boxes. The liner seemed to be Swedish, but all the passengers were German, and the lyric growl of German was everywhere on the air.

At the far corner, just where the German travellers entered, was a table with a couple of frail elderly women. The sign on their table advertised bush-walks. But only for people over fifty. Michael had turned fifty a couple of weeks ago, and he had not yet sampled the special delights reserved for those lucky travellers in time. The women thought he was from the liner, but he told them no. They said that every week they invited someone from another country to join them for a walk in the country. They only accepted six people, but nobody at all had applied today. Did he want to come tomorrow for a walk up a mountain?

He went. They were so pleasant, and he hadn't realized

until that moment that he was lonely and he missed Sarah. Since he had left Canada he felt unstable, floating on the surface, and he was looking for an anchor.

He found his anchor almost before the group had gathered. She didn't look remotely like she was fifty, she laughed almost incessantly, and she had spent ten years in Nanaimo. She was forty, somebody's niece just in from Sydney for the weekend, and she took Michael's hand when they were crossing a small stream on the side of a mountain. His fingers felt as if they had been set on fire. Canada was a great place to visit, she told him, but she was Australian to the core, and she didn't intend to leave the continent again. She extended her vacation for a week, and when she left for Sydney on a Monday morning, Michael was with her, as hopelessly in love as if he had been fifteen.

She was a nurse. One of the last remaining nurses in Australia, she said. The government had shut down so many hospital beds that nurses were considered an endangered species, like the Tasmanian tiger and the koala. She took Michael to her tiny flat in an area called the Grange, not far from the university. The area was full of little restaurants where you brought your own wine and they uncorked it for you.

Her name was Melba. As in Melba toast, she told Michael. As in peach Melba. Every morning, she went off to work in a hospital, and Michael took bus tours and walked around King's Cross and Circular Quay and took pictures of the Japanese at the Sydney opera house who were taking videos of him. On the weekend, Melba took him out to Bondi Beach and they watched the surfers come crashing in on the surf.

Finally, she asked him what his plans were. He'd been living with her for over a month and seemed, she said, to have no plans at all. She was right. Michael had stopped planning beyond the next day. Even that was an effort. He preferred to get up and get on a bus and see where it took him.

"I guess I'll go back to Canada," he told her. He had been dreaming of skating on the lake, white as far as you could see in any direction. "Why don't you come with me? We could get married or something."

"No," she said. "I'm staying right here. I've been in Canada long enough to know that I don't want to live there. Now, if you decided to stay in Australia, that might be a completely different thing. A carpenter can get a job anywhere."

Michael agreed to think about it for a week, but he knew by the next morning that he was not going to stay. Everything was fine in Australia, but it was only scenery. It didn't have anything to do with him.

"I'm going back," he told Melba. "But first I've got to go to the tropics. Up to Cairns and the Great Barrier Reef and the Daintree Forest. Why don't you come with me? We could have a holiday, and maybe one of us will change our mind." He remembered his promise to Billy, and he intended to fulfil it, but it wasn't something he could talk to her about.

"It'll have to be you who changes," she said. But she went anyway. She got ten days off, and they flew up to Cairns and rented a car, a little blue Daihatsu. They found a place to stay, a collection of cabins right on the beach in Yorkey's Knob, just north of Cairns. The woman from whom they rented the place called them "bures."

"Must be an Australian word," Michael said, but Melba had never heard it before either. The cabins had no windows, only metal screens, and though the days were lovely, it rained all night, every night. Coconuts and giant black beans fell from the trees onto their tin roof, and the sound was like cannon balls. It was like being shelled by artillery. Michael was worried that a coconut might fall on his head, but Melba told him that never happened, and he believed her, even though one morning they found a coconut floating in the swimming pool. He was starting to dream of snow, large soft flakes and the way light looked through them.

The days were hot, so hot that sweat poured off Michael whenever he moved, but he loved the heat. He wore a Tilley hat and smeared himself with sunblock. Everything that was different about this place reminded him of home. The sweltering rain forest made him think of cool dark spruces. The bougainvillaea reminded him of wild roses.

They went up to the Daintree River and took a tour boat past mangrove trees and crocodiles sunning themselves on banks. Thousands of flying foxes hung upside down in the trees, and when something startled them they darkened the sky, making sharp, pathetic cries. Pythons were curled in the lower branches, and the boat came so close to one that Michael thought he might have reached out and pulled it out of the tree.

Then they went up the Mossman Gorge where the air was so moist that everything, even the leaves and bark on the trees, was damp. There were warnings everywhere of the danger of swimming in the river, but it was full of swimmers nevertheless. Michael thought they might be German, though he had no reason for thinking so except that they were blond and looked in good physical health. They watched for a long time until four swimmers decided to brave the rapids. One of them, a girl of about seventeen, lost her nerve and clung to a rock. The others disappeared down the river and around a bend, and they didn't come back. A half-hour later she was still clinging to the rock. Michael shouted to her, did she need help? She said no, everything was fine, and so they left her there. On the way out, Michael went down to the rapids to feel the temperature of the water. It looked clear and cold, but it was hot, as hot nearly as the water that comes from a tap.

Michael thought he might be able to live in the tropics, but Melba wouldn't even think about it. She couldn't stand the heat and the moisture. Michael told her that one Winnipeg winter would cure all her fear of heat, but she didn't want that either. They went shopping in an air-conditioned supermarket, but neither of them liked that.

The day before the holiday was to end, they took a boat out to the Great Barrier Reef. They still hadn't worked anything out. Somewhere out at sea there was a cyclone, and the seas were heavy and churned up, so that even from the windows of the semi-submersible boat, they didn't see very much. They stopped at a tiny island called Michaelmas Cay where thousands of birds were nesting, and huge frigate birds circled over the others, waiting for a nest to be abandoned for an instant. They reminded Michael of the pictures of helicopters hovering in Vietnam. On the way back, dozens of Japanese tourists were vomiting into paper bags. Michael stood out on the deck and got wet, wondering what it would be like to fish in these waters.

The next day, Melba would fly back to Sydney. Michael's ticket would take him back to Canada. They would both leave at nine o'clock in the evening. They spent the day walking along the beach out to where a small river prevented you from going any farther. It looked like a place where you would find sea shells, but there were none. Melba wanted to see an estuary crocodile, but there were none of those either. A kookaburra flew into a tree near them and laughed at them in its mournful, crazed way. Then it flew off. Michael looked very carefully at Melba and wondered if he was really in love with her. He'd know as soon as the airplane left the ground, but by then it might be too late.

When they got back to the bure, Melba announced that she was going to take a swim in the salt-water pool. Somebody had seen an estuary crocodile in the swamp beyond the pool. She took her stuff and walked over. Michael stayed behind and read the paper. Apparently absolutely nothing had happened in Canada, though there was a considerable amount about the royal family, and in particular Charles's infidelities.

Michael didn't feel like swimming, but he decided that he'd better make use of his last chance. He put on his trunks and draped a towel over his shoulders. On the way, a Ulysses butterfly tried to alight on his hand. He identified it immediately, because he'd bought a postcard with a picture of one to take home as a souvenir. It was enormous, brilliant blue as if it were lit from inside, and Michael thought about Billy. This was what Billy had wanted, but Billy was buried under the frozen Manitoba earth. Under three feet of snow.

Melba was sitting in a deck chair reading a magazine. Michael swam the length of the pool using a slow butterfly stroke. Then he swam back with a sidestroke. He was on his way to the far end of the pool again using a lazy breaststroke when he saw them. Two brilliant green butterflies and an enormous black one with polka dots on it. Their beauty took his breath away. They danced at the edge of the forest beyond the pool. It was like watching a fire that had escaped from a fireplace and was dancing in the air. He thought to himself, I am going to remember this moment for as long as I live.

"Sure are nice, aren't they?" said a familiar voice from the edge of the pool. Billy was sitting there, his feet trailing in the water.

"You're dead," Michael said. "You are dead aren't you?"

"Well, no," Billy told him. "Not exactly. I mean, I'm officially dead as far as the government is concerned. But I'm here breathing and eating, if you see what I mean."

"No, I don't," Michael said. "I don't see what you mean at all. You are either dead or you are alive." Billy seemed fully human sitting there. Nothing about him seemed at all like a ghost, and Michael didn't believe in ghosts anyway.

"It's a remission," Billy said. "The cancer went into remission, and so I came here. That sure is a beautiful girl you've got with you."

"Melba," Michael told him.

"Yes, I know. I was talking to her earlier. You know, Michael, I never got married because I could never find the right girl. Now this is exactly the girl I wanted to marry. She tells me you're going back to Canada. That true?"

"Yes. My plane leaves at nine o'clock."

"Then I suppose you won't be upset if I marry her?"

"Have you asked her to marry you?"

"No, no. I've hardly met her. But I'm going back to Sydney, and if you have no objections, I'd like to court her."

Michael looked over at the far end of the pool. The butterflies were still dancing, still as beautiful as before. "No," he told Billy. "You go ahead. But you'll never get her to leave Australia and come to Canada."

"No," Billy agreed, "she can't." A Ulysses butterfly drifted over and landed on Billy's shoulder, a brilliant blue patch. He didn't seem to notice. Michael turned to where the other butterflies had been dancing, but they were gone, and when he turned back to Billy, he was gone as well.

All the way to the airport, they hardly spoke until Melba said, "Well, I guess that's it."

"Yes," Michael said. "Do you regret it?"

"No," Melba said. "It wasn't a thing that had a future. It was just something that happened." Her flight was a few minutes later than his, and she had seen him to the gate.

He kissed her goodbye and just as he was going through the gate to security, he called out to her, "Take good care of Billy."

"What?" she called. "What did you say?" But Michael was already too far away to answer. He followed a crowd of people onto the airplane and found his seat. All the way to Hawaii, and all the way from Hawaii to Vancouver, and all the way from Vancouver to Winnipeg the flight was as smooth as a butterfly.